The Estranged Photographer

RAELYN SHAYE

Gotham Books

30 N Gould St.
Ste. 20820, Sheridan, WY 82801
https://gothambooksinc.com/

Phone: 1 (307) 464-7800

© 2025 *Raelyn Shaye*. All rights reserved.

No part of this book may be reproduced, stored in a retrieval system, or transmitted by any means without the written permission of the author.

Published by Gotham Books (April 22, 2025)

ISBN: 979-8-3485-8126-8 (P)
ISBN: 979-8-3485-8127-5 (E)

Because of the dynamic nature of the Internet, any web addresses or links contained in this book may have changed since publication and may no longer be valid.

The views expressed in this work are solely those of the author and do not necessarily reflect the views of the publisher, and the publisher hereby disclaims any responsibility for them.

Chapters

1. 1
2. 11
3. 20
4. 30
5. 40
6. 49
7. 58
8. 67
9. 76
10. 86
11. 95
12. 104
13. 113
14. 122
15. 131
16. 140
17. 150
18. 159
19. 168
20. 177

1

He walked freely on the streets. Passing potential victims along the way. *Did he look?* No. Not needing to look, he could smell the right victim as he passed by them. Keeping to himself, he didn't stand out in a crowd. Other than the ones that were killed, he avoided confrontation with people. Obviously, no one would know the type of person he was. His name was Tim. He was middle-aged, tall with blonde hair, and didn't keep up with his appearance at times.

He would be cautious with every step he took during his journey of killings. Planning thoroughly a short time before attacking his victims, Tim stalked women without being known. After a few hours of watching, he went in for the prize. Nothing could stop him from fulfilling his goal of murder.

Most of the trophies were in his head collected from the years of his work. He kept nothing physically from the victims, but everything mentally. Tim kept a one-track mind during his killings. One snapshot of the girls was made with posed perfection and hidden at his trophy graveyard in the woods back home. Tim's evil soul ran deep with a heart full of corruption. His mind filled with immoral thoughts. The past haunted him tremendously. Reflecting on his life only made things worse. With the heartaches, he focused on how to make them disappear. Killing was his way to forget. *Could he find other ways to heal besides killing?*

A professional photographer who killed women during his jobs in different states is who he was. Tim Traveled quite a bit to a variety of tourist attractions and events. Taking pictures for his own personal art gallery or parties such as weddings, graduations at schools, and more. Whatever job he could get into when it came to photography. He worked for a company that sent him everywhere. He stayed gone for several weeks to oversee projects at times. This is what he loved to do. It gave him peace from his scarce home life.

Disappearing on occasion to do his killings, he was careful not to leave evidence that would trace anything back to himself. Tim didn't choose the victims that he worked with or around. It would have been too suspicious. He has a good and bad side to him. His good side is gentle, quiet, calm, weak, and collective. Something that would appear normal to others around him. His bad side is rough, evil, impulsive, strong, and hurtful. Tim was from a small town out west. His mom worried about him all the time, even though he lived around the corner from his parents. Woods surrounded the town with not a lot of things to do.

Tim always had trouble finding a girlfriend. Dating rarely, girls found him odd. Back in his younger days, he had little friends. Everyone picked on him and said he was different. So, he kept to himself a lot. No one knew the pain he dealt with on a daily basis.

This would even stay hidden from his family. He left the house to venture through the woods by himself. Tim enjoyed being one with nature. Spending his days alone wasn't fun. Especially when he could hear other children playing in the distance. Their laughter brought sadness to Tim. He wished someone would be a true friend.

His first killing was when he was a kid. Tim played spin the bottle with so-called friends one evening and experienced a kiss.

"What are you waiting for?" Derek said.
"Kiss her." Zoe hollered.

Tim went in for the kiss. After, it felt awkward to him and the other kids laughed as he stood there aroused. His body was going through things that he didn't quite understand yet. The girl he kissed even laughed. Tim ran off embarrassed. Later, he saw the girl walking alone and killed her. The case went cold. Tim never feared getting caught and became thirsty for more. He felt a satisfaction from it. It was a way for him to release all of the anger he held inside.

A few years later, he killed again. This time he was out of town while visiting family with his parents. His cousins took him out to the caves where there was a party. After a while, Tim wanted to leave. With Tim not being a social person, he wasn't enjoying himself much.

"You seem lonely." Amber said.
"I don't party much. I was just about to leave." Tim explained.
"I can walk you home." Amber said.
"If you want." Tim responded.
"Okay, come on." She said.

No one saw them leave. They were busy drinking and having fun. The two slipped off into the darkness together. Her, never to be seen again. Tim grew angry when the girl tried to kiss him. He turned on her almost instantly, killing her with his own hands. Skeletal remains were found years later and the girl was identified. Everyone at the party was questioned. Just like the first case, it went unsolved. If only others knew how dangerous Tim was, they could have a chance to protect themself.

When Tim finally did meet the girl he wanted, they married. She became pregnant shortly after. Life had seemed to be perfect for Tim until one saddened moment. His wife went into early labor and he rushed her to the hospital. The doctors did all they could, but couldn't save either one of them. Tim lost his wife and child at birth. Turned out, his wife had an unknown stomach issue that caused her to miscarry.

Afterward, Tim became lonely and depressed. He held on to the hatred of what life handed him and became unaware of his surroundings at times. He thought his killing days were over when he married. He would take the secret to his own grave. Things took a turn for the worse when he was alone once more.

He couldn't handle the thought of losing his only true love. He would have trouble trying for another relationship. Instead, his mind went back to where it was before he met the woman of his dreams.

He thought his traveling job would be a fix to his problems, but it only gave him more opportunity in the end. He would become known as the estranged photographer. Tim's days were longer than other people and time was passed with thoughts of revenge on the world. The perfect job Tim found after the loss of his family. Being a photographer who traveled for business. *What else could be better?*

This would take him away from the disturbing life he knew at home and take him out into a whole new world of possibilities. At first, everything went fine.

Then, he began having urges to hurt others as he passed by happy couples. Seeing them together only grew more hatred over time. *Could he control himself?*

He chose girls randomly wherever he went. When he smelled a good victim, he turned to follow. Tim quickly learned about them through his six senses. Then, when isolated, he lunged for the grab. Once he went in, it became all satisfaction. His mind left the world around him as he embraced his killings. First, the choke. Second, the pose. After, the kill. The fear from the victims had greatly exceeded his expectations. He needed to have more.

The cravings grew stronger with each killing. Nothing would stop him from having his victory. He hurt without thought. He reacted with compulsive behavior. Tim was another person with multiple personalities. Coming back to reality when finished, he made sure nothing was left. Leaving bodies at the crime scenes before exiting quietly, Tim made his way back to the hotels he stayed at.

He tried talking to women a few times, but they would laugh at him or be rude. So, he walked on. On occasion, one would go on a date with him. He wanted badly to get out of the killings. It never worked. Every time a girl hurt his heart, Tim went back into revenge mode in his mind. Eventually, another girl would have to pay the price for each rejection that came.

With one of his killings, Tim waited till she entered the dark alley. Then, approached her slowly from behind. The grab around the neck was rough as he covered her mouth with his hand. She tried to scream while being pulled into an abandoned building. Once inside, he choked her. Not killing her, but just enough to put her to sleep. When she awoke, her mouth was taped shut with her hands tied to a pole.

Tim admired her in the darkness lying naked. Her clothes were torn off and thrown across the floor. He took a picture after posing her body in a certain way. Then, strangled her to end it for good. She thought he was going to put her to sleep again. Instead, she would never awaken this time. Tim never raped his victims, and always left the crime scenes clean.

He liked to tie his women down and make them fear death. Also, he covered their mouth to muffle the noise they tried to make. Leaving the bodies where they were strangled, Tim took his tape and rope with him. Nothing was left behind. Then, Tim took his camera back to the hotel until he arrived home after his jobs were complete.

He retrieved to his dark room in the basement. When developed, he spent the night satisfying himself while admiring the photo of his latest victim. He had his own developing room. The pictures looked amazing to him as they hung to dry. The next morning, he took the picture out back of his house, deep into the woods to bury it with the rest of his treasured photos. Tim left a stump on top of the unmarked graves to remind him of each victim. He made his way back to the house where he met his mother.

"Why are u here?" Tim asked.
"I came to visit." His mother replied.
"But, why?" He asked.

She glanced at his hands.

"*Your hands are dirty.*" His mother stated.

Tim stared into his mother's eyes.

"*What was you doing back in the woods?*" His mother asked.
"*I walk the trails. I fell and got my hands dirty.*" Tim replied.
"*Are you okay?*" His mother asked.
"*I will be fine.*" Tim replied as he walked into the house.
"*Let me make you breakfast.*" His mother said as she followed.
"*I don't have time. I have another job to do. I will grab food on the way.*" Tim explained.
"*Okay, I will come back some other time.*" His mother responded as he left.

Tim's mother stood at the kitchen window for a while before leaving. She couldn't understand why her son liked the woods so much. Something seemed off to her, but she couldn't quite put her finger on it. She noticed how weird her son began acting after the death of his wife. *Would she ever find out the truth about her son?*

One day, Tim received a phone call from his mother. His dad was in the hospital and not doing well. It was something he didn't expect to hear. Taking a little time off work wasn't what Tim wanted, but he went to his dad's bedside. It was too late. The doctors said his dad had died moments before. It was a heart attack.

"*Tell my wife and child I love them.*" Tim whispered in his dad's ear.

Tim sat and cried a few tears before leaving.

"Where are you going?" Tim's mom asked as he was leaving the room.

Tim turned to his mother.

"Home." He replied.
"I'll be there later." His mother stated.
"No." Tim said quickly.
"Why not?" His mother asked.

Tim turned to walk away.

"I want to be alone." He replied.
"Tim..." His mother said.

Tim kept walking. Later that evening, he found himself reflecting back on life. He couldn't help but think his wife and child were looking down on him disappointed. Tim had done several killings that began before meeting his wife. She never knew, but he was sure she knew now. He felt a little remorse for his victims at that moment. Tim honestly wanted to stop killing. He just didn't know how. With all the anger he held inside, it was the only relief he had. Surely his wife could understand. Tim dried his tears and was determined to change his ways. He wanted his child to be proud. *Could Tim change?* His mother decided to visit the next morning.

"Why are you here." Tim asked.
"I came to check on you." His mother replied.
"I am fine." Tim stated.

He began to shut the door.

"Do you want to help me plan the funeral?" His mother asked.

"No. Let your sister help you." Tim replied as he shut the door.

Suddenly, his mother opened the door and walked in.

"Why do you treat me this way?" His mother asked.

Tim turned around to his mother.

"You need to leave." Tim said.
"No! You are going to talk to me Tim." His mother responded.

Facing his mother, Tim stared into her eyes.

"Well, answer me." His mother said.
"You don't think I know?" Tim asked.
"Know what?" His mother asked.
"Stop playing dumb." Tim replied.

He walked into the kitchen with his mother following.

"What are you talking about?" His mother asked in curiosity.
"I know about the affairs!" Tim yelled out as he looked at his mother.

Tim's mother teared up. She wasn't aware he knew what she had done. She wasn't sure how to explain it.

"How much do you know?" His mother asked.
"I saw you sneak different men in." Tim replied.
"It isn't what you think." His mother said.
"Then explain." Tim responded.

His mother sighed. I don't know how to tell you this.

"Just tell me the truth." Tim said.

The guys you seen were from the agency.

"What agency?" Tim asked.
"The adoption agency." His mother replied.
"I'm adopted?" Tim asked with confusion.
"Not exactly." His mother replied.
"Tell me the truth." Tim said.
"Your father and I couldn't conceive the natural way, so we had them take my eggs and put in your father's sperm." His mother explained.

Tim looked at his mother with relief for a moment.

"So, I'm still your child." Tim responded.
"Mine, yes. I found out later that they had a mix up with the sperm and put a different guy's semen in me. I never told your father. They found out who your donor was and came to let me know. It was a back-and-forth thing for a while." His mother continued.
"Who is my father?" Tim asked.

His mother turned away.

"Who is my father?" Tim asked again.
"He ended up in prison." His mother replied.
"For what?" Tim asked.
"Rape and murder of three girls." His mother replied.

It was like life had slapped him in the face. Now Tim knew why he had such urges to hurt people. It was heredity. He had a killer's blood.

"I didn't want to tell you. I would have taken it to my grave." His mother said.

Tim felt relief for the first time since the death of his child. It made him happy he had not passed down the killer's blood to his own. His mother eventually left to go make funeral arrangements. Later that night, Tim unscrambled his thoughts. A lot made sense to him now. He just needed to figure out how to stop it, how to fix his urges without his family ever knowing what he did.

After the funeral, Tim went back to his job. His mother wanted him to take off longer, but he didn't want to stay at home. Even more determined not to kill, Tim tried to keep his mind on the job. The only problem was that he still saw the happy moments between couples. He had longed for another relationship. *Could Tim find what he needed?*

The more Tim saw happy couples, the more he grew angry. Life wasn't fair in his eyes. *Would it ever be?*

2

Tim smelled yet another victim as she passed him. He quickly turned around to follow. She went into a few stores as he stood outside and waited. Once she began down a dark road, he went for the attack. She was a fighter. Someone he struggled to control. He eventually overpowered her by hitting her to the point of knocking her out. She lay bleeding on the street. He saw a big rock and hit her one last time, killing her. This one was too risky to mess with, so he walked away. Stopping at a creek in the woods to clean up before returning to the hotel he was staying at. *What went wrong?*

No one had ever before fought as much as she. Not liking this, Tim knew he had to find another. The sirens of the police went off. This meant someone found the woman he left in the street. Staying low, he didn't want to raise suspicion. Instead, he thought of the mistakes he made.

"I should have been tighter on my hold." He whispered to himself.

Not wanting to go home empty-handed, he rested for the night to regain his power. Tim was determined to get another victim for his graveyard. Memories of his marriage overwhelmed his thoughts. This angered him more. Life had given him a chance to be happy without feeling the need to kill. Then, in one day, life took it all away. The whole situation was confusing to Tim. He had wondered at one point if life would ever bring him such an opportunity again.

The following evening, he walked for miles around town before finding his next victim. Finally, his smell triggered as he passed a young woman. Instantly, he began following her. It was dark out, in the middle of the night. He had little time to react.

The first opportunity came when the woman entered a ball field at the edge of town. He waited until she was halfway across before sneaking behind her for the grab. His arm wrapped around her throat, his other hand over her mouth. He put her to sleep in the field. Then, dragged her to a tree where no one could see them together.

She began to wake up, but not before Tim tied her to a tree. As she opened her eyes, he could see the fear in her.

"Is she wondering what I am going to do next?" Tim thought to himself.

The fear only excited him more.

"Let me go." She whispered.

Tim walked around her slowly before kneeling beside her. Leaning to the side of her face, he smelled her scent.

"I can't" He softly said.

She closed her eyes tightly. In fear, she avoided staring at him the best she could.

"What are you going to do to me?" She asked.
"I'm going to kill you." He replied.
"But why? What did I do to you?" She asked.

Tim only looked at her in the moment. This would be the first time he had a conversation with a victim. *Would this change the outcome?* He quickly grabbed the tape.

"No! Don't! Just let me go!" She hollered out.
"Shut up!" Tim whispered loudly while throwing tape over her mouth.

Before standing back up, he ripped her clothes off throwing them across the ground. She tried to fight it, but being tied to a tree made it hard. Tim admired her naked body for a few minutes while watching her cry in fear. Wanting to rape her, he had to keep his composure. Reminding himself not to leave any evidence. Her body was almost irresistible. He eventually went in for the death choke. Watching her as she lost consciousness, he was content. These moments were what he lived for and the relief he needed inside. A moment where he controlled life. After posing her body, he took his picture. Then, left before daylight leaving no trace behind him.

The next day Tim returned home where he spent time in his basement developing again. There was one problem. He was interrupted by his mother. The sounds of footsteps coming down the stairs, startled him. He turned around angrily at his mother.

"What are you doing down here?" Tim asked.
"I wanted to talk to you." His mother replied.
"You know this is where I do my work. You are not supposed to be coming down here!" Tim hollered as he quickly pulled his mom back upstairs.
"Calm down Tim!" His mother hollered back.

Tim stared at his mother in anger.

"Maybe you should go see a therapist for all the anger you have built up inside." His mom suggested.
"Oh, now you are concerned about me." Tim sarcastically said.
"You don't mean that." His mom said surprisingly.

Both angrily stared.

"What do you want?" Tim asked.
"I came to check on you. I was worried about you after our last conversation." His mother replied.

"I am fine." He said.
"You lost your family, your dad died. Are you really fine Tim?" His mom asked.

Tim instantly stood in front of his mother's face.

"Don't ever bring up my family again!" Tim hollered.
"I'm sorry. I-" His mom said before she was interrupted.
"And as far as my dad is concerned, well, we both know the truth to that." Tim stated.

His mother glanced with shock.

"That was no one's fault. He has always been your father. The nerve..." Tim's mom said.
"The nerve?" Tim asked.
"What?" His mother asked in confusion.
"You were the one that kept the lie from us both!" Tim yelled.
"I did it to protect you." His mom said.
"Protect me from what? The truth of my own blood?" Tim asked in anger.
"You're not like him. You are not a murderer" His mom replied.

Tim stood in silence. It took everything he had in him to not show his mother differently. If only she knew the truth this time. What she had caused. Tim could have had help for his issues a long time ago, but his mother thought it would best to keep quiet. Tim might have had a better outcome, if he could have had a better understanding of why he felt the urge to hurt people. The answer was quite clear. It was in his blood. Little did he know, he came from a killer's blood. *Was this information fair to be kept from Tim?* He didn't think so. Tim thought his mother should have told him the truth. He had every right to know where he belonged. Tim's mother never knew about his urges to kill. He was always afraid to tell her, so he kept quiet.

"I think you should leave now." Tim stated.
"I want to fix this." His mom said.
"There is no fixing this now." Tim responded.

His mother looked confused.

"What do you mean, Tim?" She asked.
"Just leave!" Tim yelled.

His mother couldn't understand why Tim was being so hostile toward her. He was going to leave her in confusion like she did him growing up. In Tim's eyes, it was clear whose fault it was for his life being the way it was. It was time his mother got a taste of her own medicine. She would have to figure it all out on her own. Tim had very little sympathy for her at this point. His mother should have never kept the secret. She left quietly, more worried than she was before. She didn't know how to help her son because he wouldn't tell her what was wrong. He had no plans to tell her either. *Would this create a bigger problem?*

Tim continued his day as usual. After burying the photo, he went back to the house to clean up. The doorbell suddenly rang.

"Who is it now?" He thought to himself.

He opened the door to find a dinner basket with a note attached to it. Picking it up to bring it inside, Tim opened the note.

"I'm sorry for everything. Please enjoy this delicious meal I prepared for you. Love, Mom."

If he hadn't been so hungry, Tim would have tossed it in the garbage. He sat at the table and ate everything his mother sent in the basket. Then, went to bed. Tim thought he should have probably thanked his mom, but wasn't going to under the circumstances. Instead, he drifted off to sleep thinking about the beautiful victim he had just killed earlier. He needed more like her, without conversation next time.

Leaving back out on the job the next morning, Tim was eager to get back to his killings. No time was wasted after completing his work. It was late as he strolled the streets in the darkness. After a while, Tim noticed he had wandered a little out of town. As he glanced around, a graveyard caught his eye. Fearlessly, he approached it slowly.

"I must have really been in thought to come this far." Tim whispered to himself.

The graveyard looked old. Something from an earlier time era. Small, chipped headstones mostly covered the yard. He couldn't help but think back to his little victim graveyard.

"I wonder how these people died? Were they murdered or was it natural causes?" He asked himself.

All of a sudden, Tim heard a noise behind him. He turned quickly to look. There was raccoon staring at him as if it were ready to attack. Its eyes were big and glowed red, startled by this, Tim grabbed a stick and swung it at the raccoon. It then ran off into the darkness. Tim usually wasn't afraid of anything, but the animal didn't look right to him. After a while in the graveyard, Tim heard another noise. This time it came from the street. As he turned around once more, Tim seen a car stopped on the side of the road. Observing, there was a woman in the car by herself.

"What is she doing out here this late?" He questioned.

Her car appeared to be broken down in front of the graveyard.

"Should I kill her?" He questioned more.

Usually, Tim picked his victims, but this time he felt fate had brought this one to him.

"It seems she is in the wrong place at the worst time." Tim assumed.

Would Tim take this random opportunity to kill? Tim thought about it. He never liked killing randomly. It was something he treasured. That night, he decided to go for the unthinkable. Maybe life was showing him other ways to get new victims, was his mindset.

"I'm going for it." Tim claimed as he started toward her.

The woman exited her car to begin walking. Tim followed closely in the dark. A few times she stopped to turn around.

"Who's there?" She called out, but no answer.

She appeared to be a little frightful of the dark.

"She seems perfect. Her smell is beautiful." Tim thought as he got closer.

Waiting for the right moment, he eventually went for the attack. This caught the woman by surprise. She tried to fight, but he was too strong. Her only option was to scream.

"Help! Somebody, please, help me!" She yelled out, but no one was close enough to hear her.

The moment came, he put her out. There she lay lifeless on the side of the road. Tim pulled her back to the graveyard where he tied her to a headstone. Admiring her after ripping the clothes off. Again, he wanted so badly to rape her. The memories of being with his wife haunted him. He thought about this for some time. Daylight would soon approach, so a decision would need to be made.

"I can have sex with her and bury her. No one would know."

She began waking up. Tim slowly lay on top of her.

"What are you doing?" She asked.
"Shh..." Tim whispered in her ear as he raped her slowly.

The woman let him do what he wanted without fighting. She assumed he would rape her and let her go if she cooperated. Afterward, Tim stood up feeling at ease.

"You are an amazing person, just like my wife." Tim stated.
"If you are married, then why do you need me?" The woman asked.

At that moment Tim was brought back into reality. He observed his surroundings for a few minutes. He found some sticks and started digging through the dirt.

"What are you doing now?" She asked.
"I'm digging a grave." Tim replied.
"Please don't kill me. I gave you what you wanted." The woman pleaded.
"I have to kill you or I will be exposed." Tim responded.
"I won't tell anyone, I promise." The woman continued to plea.
"I can't trust you." Tim said as he continued to dig.
"Go home to your wife." She said.

Stopping to glance at the woman,

"My wife is dead!" He yelled.
"Did you kill her too?" She asked in confusion.

Tim suddenly choked the woman, killing her.

"No, I would have never killed her." He said as he finished digging the grave.

Afterward, he untied her and pushed her into the hole. Then, threw the dirt on top of her until she was completely underground. Tim took her clothes and threw them into her car. Putting the car in neutral, he pushed it about a mile farther out of town next to a creek bed. Setting it on fire with old techniques he had learned in the past, he didn't want anything coming back to him. He was sure to be careful.

The police found the car, but it was too burnt to uncover any evidence. They had assumed the driver lost control and was in the river somewhere. The stream was strong, so it could have carried a person down to the river waters. No other proof gave them any suspicion of something else.

Tim was exhausted from this kill. He thought it was too difficult and risky to do anything like that again. He would go back to his normal killing ways. With all the extra he was required to do, he had forgotten to take the picture. This would be a killing that he kept mentally to himself. He traveled home, where he stayed a few days to rest.

3

His mother visited over the next few days, cooking and cleaning for him even though Tim often found this annoying.

"Your laundry is folded." She said.
"You don't have to be here doing anything." Tim responded.
"I just want to help. You look exhausted." His mom stated.
"I'm fine." Tim said as he sat at the table.
"I brought you something." She said.

His mother brought him a plate of food. Tim began to eat. He was hungrier than he thought.

"See, you were hungry." She said.

Tim looked at her as he took another bite. Maybe she was right. He finished his food and went to rest more. A while later, he woke up and started packing things for work the next day.

"Are you leaving so soon?" His mother asked.
"You are still here?" Tim asked back.

His mother was eager for her son to stay.

"Take a few more days off. Let me take care of you." She responded.
"I have to go do a job tomorrow." Tim said.
"When will you come back?" She asked in curiosity.
"A few days." He replied.

Not wanting to anger him, she went along with what he wanted.

"Okay, I will come and help you when you get back." She stated.

"I don't need your help." He quickly responded.

In the moment, she grew confident.

"I'm your mother and I will always be around whether you like it or not." His mom said.

Tim stared at her with confidence thinking,

"So, you think."

His jobs were complete within a week. He took on a couple of them in one area. It was a big money maker for him. He decided to take a walk around town. While enjoying the night stroll, Tim saw a woman sitting outside her window on the second floor of the fire escape. She was beautiful to him. Trying to avoid her, he kept walking past the apartment building. He didn't want to appear suspicious.

"Maybe I should go back to the hotel now. I don't feel the urge to kill this one." Tim whispered in the night air.

What he wanted to do, was go back to the woman. The beauty she presented was hard to forget. Turning around, Tim wanted to see her one last time before heading back to the hotel for the night. He couldn't resist the thought of taking another glance up the fire escape. His urge was just to admire her. He could stand all day and stare but knew he couldn't make himself obvious.

"I will take a quick photo of her and run away." Tim claimed.

When he arrived at the apartments, the woman was gone. He also noticed her lights were out. She had decided to go to bed, but her window was still ajar. Standing by the fire escape steps, he thought for a while.

"I can climb through her window and watch her sleep. She would never know I was there." Tim convinced himself.

That's what he did. Tim climbed through the woman's window. It was dark inside so he tried to be careful not to make noise. Once he entered the bedroom, he could see the woman sleeping. It was a warm night, so she had little on. She looked perfect in Tim's eyes. The urges inside him began growing intensely. Eventually, he could barely hold back. The time had come for him to leave. He didn't want to take this one too far. As his urges grew, he stepped into the darkness.

"I need to leave now or I am going to rape her. She's too beautiful for my eyes." Tim said to himself.

Tim made himself leave that night. Something about her he liked and didn't want to hurt her. This was out of the ordinary for Tim to think in this way. When she was sitting on that window balcony, he could see the sadness in her eyes. This is something he connected with right away. She wasn't happy like the other women he seen. It was different.
He wondered what could make her feel down. He slept the whole night before going to a diner for breakfast the next morning. After seating himself, a waitress came to take his order. It was her. The beautiful, sad woman from the night before.
Tim couldn't believe his eyes as he watched her approach the table. This made him nervous.

"Hi, my name is Ava, I'll be your server." She said.

Tim admired her for a moment.

"Hi." Tim responded.

Things appeared awkward between them.

"What would you like today?" She asked.
"I'll take the breakfast special and a cup of coffee." Tim finally answered.
"I will have that right out to you." She responded.

After a long few minutes, she returned with his food and coffee. She set the plate down but her arm hit the cup, spilling it all over Tim. Ava quickly grabbed napkins. She was embarrassed.

"I'm so sorry sir!" Ava said in distress as she tried to clean the coffee off Tim.

Tim found this to be funny, but Ava was confused.

"Sir, you are laughing." Ava said.
"Please, call me Tim. I couldn't get mad at such a beautiful woman as you." Tim responded.

They both looked at each other silently as she cleaned up the coffee mess. This made her nervous.

"I get off at eight tonight if you want to hang out. I feel like I owe you for dumping coffee in your lap." Ava said.
"You don't owe me anything. I will come anyway." Tim said.

Tim couldn't wait to meet back with her. This excited him as much as it did to be with his wife. When the time finally came, he was waiting outside the diner. Ava walked out around eight just like she said. She glanced over to see Tim waiting on her. Not expecting him to show, she approached him slowly.

"I didn't think you would show." Ava claimed.
"Surprise." Tim said sarcastically.
"Okay, a sarcastic man you are." Ava said.
"So, what are we doing?" Tim asked.
"Follow me." She replied.

They went back to her apartment. She had brought dinner from work for the two of them. It was the least she could do for him after giving him a coffee bath at breakfast. The two ate together and talked. Tim wanted to know more about her sadness. He wasn't sure if she would talk about it. Later that evening,

"Why do you seem so sad sometimes?" Tim asked.
"My boyfriend and I broke up. I caught him cheating on me with another woman." Ava replied.
"You are beautiful. It's his loss." Tim responded

They embraced in a kiss. It never stopped there. The bedroom was where the two ended up. For the first time in a long time, Tim made passionate love to a woman without the thought of hurting her. He could enjoy himself. The next morning, she ran out the door to work. Tim went back to the hotel. The thoughts of Ava overwhelmed his mind. He decided to take extra time to stay around for her. It brought happiness to his world when they were together. He needed to keep seeing her. She was amazing.

Over the next week, the two spent a lot time together. Tim was in love. His wife was the only other person that made him feel this way. One night,

"Ava, I think I have fallen in love with you." Tim said.

Ava sighed.

"We need to talk." She said softly.

Tim looked confused. This didn't sound good to him. *What could she possibly want to tell him?*

"About what?" He asked.
"My ex-boyfriend called and apologized. He wants me back." Ava replied.
"But, what about us?" Tim asked with worry.
"I like you a lot, but I have a history with him." Ava replied with sorrow.

Tim thought on this for a minute.

"Would you consider giving us a chance?" Tim asked.
"I love him." Ava replied.

Tim couldn't believe what was happening. He thought they were good together. He didn't want to lose her.

"Do you have feelings for me?" Tim asked.
"Yes, but I'm not over him yet." Ava replied.
"I can help you with that." He said.

Ava wasn't sure what to say.

"You can move in with me. I'll take care of you. He won't know where you are." Tim explained.
"Tim, I can't do that right now. I'm sorry." Ava responded.

This was not something Tim wanted to hear. He loved Ava and wanted nothing more. This upset him. He left without saying another word. Sitting in his hotel room, Tim couldn't stop thinking about Ava. Anger grew inside him once again as he strolled the streets passing happy couples. Stopping at a gas station for something to drink, a woman caught his eye. He waited outside for her to leave. Tim had the urge to kill. Nothing could stop it at this point. His sadness overpowered him. Someone had to pay the price for his pain.

The woman exited the station and began walking through an alley. Tim went in for the attack. She was put to sleep with the tightening of his arm around her throat. With no rope to tie her, he needed to think fast. He pulled her behind the dumpster, ripped her clothes off, and posed her for a quick picture. After taking the photo, she started to wake up. Tim knelt beside her. This kill had to happen fast before she yelled and he was caught.

"I'm sorry for this, but you have to die now." Tim whispered to her.

The woman became frightened and tried to get up, but Tim pulled her back to the ground where he choked her to death. Then, he ran off into the darkness. He stopped at another station down the road to wash his face. It was hot and he needed to cool off. This cleared his head enough to get back to the hotel. After checking out of the hotel, he returned home. Tim made sure he never took jobs in the same town he killed in. Never wanting anyone to recognize him, he would stay away so he wasn't caught for the killings.

Arriving home, he met his mother at the door.

"Where have you been?" His mom asked.
"Will you stop treating me like I'm a child!" Tim hollered as he went inside the house.
"You are my child and I was worried about you." His mother responded following him.

Tim set his stuff down and turned to his mother.

"I am fine." He said.
"You were gone a long time." His mother claimed.
"I was working." Tim responded.

A few seconds later,

"That was a long job." She said.
"Please, stop." He said.

Tim began to walk away.

"I will cook you dinner." She said.
"I'm not hungry." He claimed.

Becoming worried,

"You have to eat." She said.
"Fine, I'll be down in a minute." Tim said as he went to his bedroom.

At dinner, his mother wanted to talk more.

"Move in with me." She said.

He glanced at his mother.

"What?" Tim asked in confusion.
"You heard me." She said.
"I am not moving in with you." Tim said as he continued to eat.
"Why not?" She asked.

Trying to hold his grip together, Tim politely replied back to his mother without yelling.

"Because I'm not giving up the memories here." He replied.

"Then I will move in with you." She said.

Tim looked at his mother once more.

"No!" Tim yelled.
"I'm here all the time anyway." His mother said.
"I know, you need to stay home more." Tim responded.

His mother decided to try and convince her son.

"If I move in here, you can slow down with work and relax more." She explained.
"I like working and being away from home." Tim claimed.
"Why?" She asked.

Now, Tim was really annoyed.

"Because I do! I'm not moving in with you and you are not moving in with me!" He yelled as he got up from the able.

Tim didn't like how his mother thought of him like a child. He was very independent and knew how to take care of himself. Trying to take over his life was not Tim's idea of a good mother. An hour later, Tim headed out the door.

"Where are you going now?" His mom asked.
"I'm going for a run. I'll be back later." Tim replied.

Tim needed time to himself.

"Okay." She said as he left.

Back in the woods, Tim visited his graveyard. He reflected on each of his killings as he sat in silence. Nothing except the sounds of nature were heard around him. This is what he enjoyed to calm his mind. With everything that was going on around him,

Tim planned to take the next week off. Since he loved nature so much, he decided to take a camping trip.

"Maybe it will help calm my mind more and I need to keep my distance from my mother." Tim thought to himself.

This trip may have been a good idea for Tim at the moment. He would have to hurry so his mother wouldn't see him leaving this time. Tim did love his mother, but was mad at her for how life turned out for him. He wasn't sure if he could completely forgive her for that reason. She had longed for a better relationship with her son, but couldn't get one.

4

Tim rushed back to the house. His mother wasn't in sight.

"Good, she isn't here." He thought.

He packed enough things for a week and left out the door. Tim was almost finished loading his car, when,

"Where are you going?" His mother asked.

Looking up to see his mother, Tim wasn't happy.

"Why are you leaving?" She asked.
"I'm going camping." Tim replied.

Becoming curious, his mother wanted to know more. She didn't like her son keeping any secrets.

"Where?" She asked.
"Does it matter?" He asked in return.

Tim's mother grew concerned. She was trying to create a better bond with her son, but it seemed like everything she did made it worse. *What else could she do to make her son love her?*

"Let's go together." She suggested.
"No." He answered quickly.
"I like camping." She said.

Tim finished his loading and walked into the house to grab his keys. His mother followed while he tried to ignore her.

"It would be great for us both to spend the alone time together." She said.

"No, it wouldn't." Tim said as he left out the door again.

His mother ran after him.

"It would be like the old days when we camped before." She pleaded.

He turned to look at her.

"I'm grown now." Tim stated.

"Adults camp together too." His mother said as she held to his arm.

"Mom, stop!" He yelled as he pulled his arm away.

She stood in sadness as he got into his car.

"Why do you push me away so much?" His mother asked as he started his car.

Tim glanced out the window at his mother.

"Why did you lie to me my whole childhood?" He asked.

She watched him drive away. She realized that maybe the secret had destroyed the relationship with her son. What she thought was best at the time, probably wasn't the best for either of them. *Is this fixable?*

Driving far, Tim found a camping spot in the next state. It was a big city town with a lot of people. He blended with the people around him. The festival was in town, so more travelers came through than usual. The campgrounds were full, but Tim found a place deep in the woods near a campground to spend a few nights. Loving nature, he wasn't picky on where to sleep. With his car parked on a deserted path at the edge of town, no one would notice he was back in the woods. He spent a few nights observing and relaxing. Being able to see the campground below him, he watched as the campers were laughing and enjoying themselves.

Tim eventually came out of hiding to walk around town. It was crowded with lots to do. Even though Tim wasn't a fan of a big crowd, he still managed to keep himself together. Nothing out of the ordinary would he show. He stopped a couple of places and ate before going back into hiding. The next day, he saw more of the festival. No killing had been on his mind since he had arrived in the new town. Enjoying himself was his goal. *Would he change his mind?*

One evening right before dark, Tim decided to take a hike on a trail in the woods that surrounded his camp. An object caught his eye. It was a piece of wood lying in the middle of the path. To his surprise, the wood was in the shape of a heart. He grew curious in the moment.

"Someone must have dropped this." He thought to himself.

Observing it, Tim slowly picked it up. This took him back to when his wife was alive. In her spare time, she painted. One of the paintings was a wooded path. She knew how he loved nature and hiking. A heart-shaped rock leads the path in the picture. *Was Tim's belated wife trying to tell him something?* Tim was upset by the memory.

"Why did you have to take her?" He cried out.

A few moments later, Tim stood up and threw the wood as far as he could into the woods. Still crying, he continued to walk. A woman from the distance was heading his way. He stood at the side of the trail hidden, silently waiting.

"She was taken from me. I will kill until someone stops me." He whispered into the air.

Tim was certain that he would never be caught. He had no hesitations when it came to killing. This was the only relief he felt from all the pain he carried. Nothing could make him feel better.

"It's a great evening for a walk."

He began to hear a conversation between two people. Hiding in the woods, he listened more. It appeared a man who was jogging along the path began interacting with the woman. Tim wasn't going to interrupt. No one knew he was a killer and the secret didn't need to be revealed quite yet. His victims were the only witnesses and they were dead. The woman became lucky at the moment.

Now, Tim had to figure out what to do. After a few moments, he decided to head back to camp. Suddenly, he heard a noise. It appeared to be another woman walking along the path. As Tim watched, he noticed the woman was the same person he had seen a few minutes prior.

"She turned around to go back." He whispered to himself.

This was Tim's chance to go in for the kill. He quietly crept up behind her. She never saw it coming. With his arm around her neck, she fell asleep. After dragging her into the woods, Tim ripped her clothes off instantly. Remembering he had nothing to tie her up with, he had to work fast.

"Dam-it!" He said.

Tim didn't have his camera. He wasn't prepared at all with this killing. *What was he going to do with her now?* Looking around, Tim noticed the heart shaped piece of wood he had thrown earlier.

"What?" He thought in silence.

He was confused as to why it had appeared again. The woman began waking up and Tim became nervous. The wood had distracted his concentration with this kill. Suddenly, he started hearing voices. Being afraid the woman would scream out, Tim grabbed the wood and hit the woman several times. Knowing this would leave evidence, he needed to come up with a plan.

"I will bury her like the woman at the graveyard." He thought.

Waiting until no one was around, Tim began digging with anything he could find around him. Once the hole was deep enough, he rolled the woman into it with all evidence. Then, he covered her with dirt.

"I have to get out of here." Tim whispered.

Night fall had arrived before Tim got back to his camp site. Finding a creek on the way back, he stopped to wash himself thoroughly. Not wanting to have anything traced back to him, he burned his clothes at camp.

"I am getting careless with my killings." Tim thought to himself.

Tim knew he needed to be careful. Not expecting to kill on this trip, he wasn't really thinking right. That was more of the moment kind of kill. Early the next morning, Tim packed up and headed home. This was a few days before expected, but he didn't want to stay after the killing. Barely making it out of the state, he decided to stop for the night. At a hotel, he would clean up more and try to redirect his mind. After a good shower, Tim went for a drive for food. It was getting late, so not much was available outside a bar environment. He found a drive thru restaurant that was closing, but they were willing to take his order.

On the way back to the hotel, Tim seen a woman alone at a park. He stopped down the road and walked toward the park area. Usually, he tried not to kill more than one in the same day, but his urges were strong. The woman was swinging slowly in deep thought. Tim wondered about her.

"What could she be thinking about." Tim said.

She was in such deep thought, she never noticed Tim coming from behind. This would be a quick, clean kill. He strangled her immediately. Then, left the scene quickly before someone saw him.

"Whatever she was thinking about, she's not anymore." Tim thought.

Come to find out, the woman was deaf. She hung at that park nightly. The police had an investigation going. It was all over the news when he returned home. After unpacking his things, Tim showered. Exiting the shower, he heard the television on. When he entered the living room, he saw his mother standing there.

"Have you seen the news?" His mother asked.

Tim walked over and turned it off.

"Why did you do that?" His mother asked.
"You don't need to be watching it." Tim replied.

Tim didn't want his mom to start becoming suspicious of him, so he preferred the television to be off as much as possible.

"There's a killer on the loose." She said.

"Let the cops handle it." He responded.
"The cops don't have a lead yet." She said.
"They will catch him sooner or later." He said.

His mother grew worried.

"You need to be careful being out there all the time." She said.
"I will be fine." He answered.
"Just be careful." She said.
"I will." He said.

Tim thought his mother worried too much. Also, she constantly tried to pry into his life. This annoyed Tim. He had wished his mother would leave him alone. She had caused enough damage in his eyes. If she didn't stop, it would push Tim over the edge. It could possibly be a bad turn out for his mother in the end.

"Let me make you something to eat." His mother said.
"I'll heat myself something to eat." Tim responded as he walked to the kitchen.
"Let me wash up your laundry then." She said following behind her son.

Tim turned around quickly toward his mother.

"Go home!" He shouted.
"No!" She shouted.
"I said GO HOME!" He screamed at her.

His mother was stunned at his loudness this time.

"I want to help you." She explained.
"For the last time, I don't need your help." Tim responded.

She was trying to have a good relationship with her son, but he wasn't interested. Tim thought the best thing she should do is to go home so he could figure things out on his own. He didn't want help from the person who lied to him. It may not have been her fault what had happened, but it was her fault for not telling him so he could get the help he needed.

"You shouldn't treat me this way." His mother stated.
"I want to relax by myself. Leave me be." Tim said.

Tim was happy that his mother finally left. After eating, he went to bed. Over the next few days, Tim stayed low. He didn't leave the house. His mother hadn't come back either. Maybe she got the hint and would stay away for a while. Tim focused on laundry, cleaning, and work stuff the time he was home. He noticed something in his bag.

"What is this?" He thought.

He pulled out an object. It was the heart shaped piece of wood.

"I thought I buried this." He said to himself.

He couldn't believe he still had the wood he used to kill his last victim.

"I must have put it in my pocket without realizing it." He thought.

Tim brought it back home not realizing what he had done.

"I have to bury it before someone finds it." He quietly said to himself.
"Bury what?" His mother asked.

Tim jumped up as he shoved the wood in his pocket. It startled him when his mother spoke.

"What are you doing here?" Tim asked angrily.
"I came to check on you." His mother replied.
"You shouldn't be here right now." He said.

His mother walked up to Tim in curiosity.

"What are you burying?" She asked.
"I don't know what you're talking about." Tim replied.
"Yes, you do." She said.
"No, I don't." He said.

She shook her head in disappointment.

"I heard you say it." She said.
"You heard me wrong!" Tim responded.
"I know what I heard." She said.
"I said you heard me wrong." Tim said.

They both stared at each other for a few moments. Tim had evil eyes on his mother, but she was too concerned to notice.

"Talk to me." His mother said.
"There's nothing to talk about." Tim said.

Tim went on about his business.

"What's wrong with you?" She asked.
"Nothing." He replied.
"Something is going on with you." She said.
"I will be leaving soon for work. You should go home now." Tim said.

She knew he wasn't going to tell her anything.

"When will you be back?" She asked.
"I'll be gone about a week." He replied.
"I wish you would talk to me." She said.

Tim ignored her.

"Well, maybe one day he will." She thought to herself.

Still curious, his mother left in silence. That evening, he found another job to travel to. Before leaving out the next morning, he went to his victim's graveyard. Sitting for a while pondering on his victims, Tim eventually buried the heart-shaped wood. It had its place in the graveyard. Tim always made sure to mark the area so he could revisit his victims.

"Now no one will find it." He whispered.

5

Coming out of the woods, Tim heard a noise in the house. He went running to see what was going on. As he entered the house, he saw his mother. There was glass all over the floor.

"What happened?" Tim asked.
"I was trying to put your dishes away and a plate slipped out of my hands." His mother replied.

Tim looked discouraged.

"Why are you putting my dishes away?" He asked.
"I was just helping." She replied.
"You don't have to do anything for me." He said.

Tim grew angry as he helped his mother clean up the mess. He had wished she would stay home more.

"Ouch!" Tim hollered.

His mother ran to him.

"Are you okay?" She asked frantically.

He shoved his mother away.

"I'm fine!" Tim hollered.
"You are bleeding." His mother said.

Looking down at his own blood, Tim began feeling an urge to hurt. He wasn't sure if he could keep himself calm for long. To avoid the conflict with his mother, he needed to leave.

"It's just a little cut. I have to go now." He said as he left out the door rushing in a hurry.

Following quickly behind him, his mother was worried in the moment. She wanted to make sure her son was alright. She would quickly realize that Tim wasn't going to stay around.

"Are you sure you will be okay?" She asked.
"Yes!" Tim replied as he jumped in his car.
"Let me clean your hand." She offered.
"I don't have time!" He said.

Tim drove off quickly. Eventually, he made his way to his next job area. Work wasn't until the next morning, so he rested for the night. He spent the next few days concentrating on work. After, he stuck around for two days in the town. One night while walking through town, Tim was approached by a woman. This wasn't an ordinary one. She wore a tight, short dress with high boots. Her hair appeared messy as Tim wondered what she wanted.

"I will give you sex for money." She said as she tried to hang on him.
"Get away from me." Tim said as he pushed her away.
"Twenty bucks." She offered.
"I said get away from me." He said.

The thought didn't interest Tim of having sex with this woman. Never before had Tim paid someone to perform any sexual activity on him. She continued trying to get Tim to say yes.

"Come on, ten bucks." She pleaded.
"I'm not interested." He responded as he walked away.
"I'll do anything you want." She said as she ran after him.

Tim turned around quickly.

"I said no!" He yelled.

She was startled by his yelling.

"Let me relieve some of that stress." She said.

He grew annoyed by the way she was pushing herself at him. Tim didn't like women touching him much unless it was someone he liked. Thinking, he decided to take matters into his own hands.

"Follow me." Tim said.
"Where are we going?" She asked.
"You said you wanted to relieve my stress." He replied.

She looked at him for a long few seconds.

"Come with me and I'll show you how my stress can be relieved." He said.

The woman seemed excited. She thought he was finally going to accept her offer. They walked into a back alley. He instantly grabbed her around the throat with no hesitation.

"You like it rough." The woman said.
"You don't know what you just got yourself into." Tim said staring into her eyes.
"What do you mean?" She struggled to ask while Tim was tightening the grip around her neck.
"You are going to die." He replied.

Tim strangled the woman to death, leaving her body lying in the alley. He never looked back.

"You should have been more careful working the streets." He said as he walked away from her lifeless body.

This killing disgusted Tim, so he didn't want a picture of her to take home. He didn't approve of the type of life she had been out living. The following day, he returned home to plan his next job run. He was there for a few days before he noticed that his mother hadn't come over. Wondering why, he called to check on her but there wasn't any answer. Then, he saw a voicemail alert on his answering machine. It was from Tim's aunt, saying his mother was in the hospital.

Feeling concerned, Tim went to visit his mother. He walked in to see her lying in a hospital bed. She appeared normal to him. Tim didn't understand what the fuss was about, but he made sure she was okay.

"What is the doctor's saying?" He asked.

His mother was surprised to see him.

"They said all my tests came back normal." She replied.
"So, nothing is wrong with you?" He said.
"They said it's stress related." She responded.
"Okay." He said.

Tim walked over observing out the window. He didn't want to be there. So, he made the visit quick.

"When are you getting released?" He asked.
"It should be today." She replied.
"Do you need a ride home?" He asked.
"My sister is taking me home and staying with me a few days." She replied.

He was relieved to hear she was doing good. Tim turned around to look at his mother.

"I'm going to be leaving for another job." He said.

His mother never liked hearing this, but she agreed.

"Okay." She said.
"I'll leave my cell phone number with Aunt in case something else happens." Tim said as he walked out the door.

His mother seemed content with Tim leaving this time. He found this odd. After leaving the hospital, Tim drove back to the house to pick his things up before leaving for work. Getting to his destination the following morning, Tim rested. He never worried about how his mother was. His aunt would call him if anything was to happen to her, so he proceeded with business.

Walking back to the hotel from a job one night, Tim noticed a woman sitting in her yard next to a pool.

"Isn't it late to be swimming?" He asked himself quietly.

Tim observed for a while longer. Staying in the distance, he didn't want to be seen.

No one else was in sight. Either she lived alone, or everyone was asleep. The longer he watched, the more his urge to kill grew. Slowly, he made his way toward the woman. Suddenly, he heard a noise to the side. Glancing over, he saw the neighbor taking the trash to the curb. Hiding in the darkness, Tim stood in silence until the man went back into his house. After waiting a few minutes longer, the neighbor finally turned his lights out and went to bed.

"That was close." Tim thought.

He had to be cautious not to be seen by anyone. Also, Tim needed to move quickly so that no one would hear the woman if she screamed out. Observing the woman again, he noticed she wasn't moving. It had looked as if she had fallen asleep on the deck by the pool. She looked peaceful lying there in the night. The stars shining above gave off little light across the sky.

Tim moved in fast and quiet. He grabbed the woman around her neck. She gasped for a breath trying to fight. Struggling to keep control, he decided to drown the woman in the pool. This was not his norm, but he had trouble strangling her with her fighting so much. Afterward, he ran off into the darkness. Tim had to leave before someone saw him. *Had Tim gotten weaker?*

No picture was taken with this out-of-character killing. Not understanding why women were overpowering him, Tim had to rethink everything. It wasn't normal for him to feel so weak. He wondered if he would be able to keep control over his victims in the future.

"What will I do if I'm not able to kill anymore?" He thought.

Questioning his abilities, Tim wasn't sure how much longer he would be able to live the killer life. When the time came for him to stop, how would he get the relief he needed from the pain he endured daily?

"I need to find weaker women." He decided.

How would Tim know which were weak? Tim had to start differentiating between women to figure out which were the stronger. He needed to pay more attention to his victims before he attacked. Returning home once again after his jobs were complete, Tim had things to figure out. Stopping at a couple of gas stations on the way, he overheard people talking.

"Did you hear about the recent victim?" A lady said.

He quickly turned to look.

"Yes, it's too close to home." Another lady replied.
"Do they know who's doing it yet?" The first lady asked.

"I heard they had a lead from one of the killings." The second lady said.

The guy clerk decided to intrude on the conversation.

"You ladies need to be careful out there." He said.

At that moment, the clerk stared at Tim.

"Anyone could be the killer." He stated.

Tim grew nervous as he paid for his stuff. Once finished, he quickly drove off. He decided he wouldn't stop anywhere else on the way home. Arriving home, Tim wanted to rest. He had a long day. Lying in bed, he thought about things he overheard. This made him concerned.

"Everyone is talking. The killings are all over the news. It's only a matter of time before I'm caught. I need to space the killings out more." He thought.

After hearing others talk about the killings, Tim decided to stop for a while until things blew over. He would have to learn to control his urges in some way. Later that evening,

"Did you hear?" A voice said.

Tim looked across the room with caution. He observed his mother and aunt standing in the doorway.

"Do you always bust into people's houses?" He asked.

They stared at each other.

"Did you hear about the latest victim that was found?" His aunt asked.

"It's all over the news, everyone knows about it." Tim replied.

His mom and sister continued to have a conversation with each other while Tim listened.

"They are saying it's different from the some of the prior killings." His mom said.
"But they still think it's the same killer." His aunt said.

Tim continued to listen more.

"Yes, how did they put it?" Mom asked.
"A killing gone wrong." They both said together.

Staring at the two, Tim was astonished.

"They think something happened that distracted the killer from his normal acts." Aunt said.

By this time, Tim had heard enough.

"You two are watching the news too much." Tim said.

Tim couldn't believe how much the two were educated about the killings. It surprised him with their knowledge. The police knew more than Tim originally thought. Now, he really needed to be careful with everything. Tim pretended to not care what they were saying.

"You two need to go home and stop listening to such things." Tim said.

They glanced over at Tim.

"We came to cook dinner for you." Aunt said.

"I have already eaten, and I'm tired." Tim responded.

His mother grew concerned.

"Are you feeling okay?" His mom said.
"Yes, I've had a long few days and need rest." He replied.

His aunt shrugged her shoulders and glanced up at Tim.

"Do you need anything before we leave?" Aunt asked.
"No." Tim replied.

The two left Tim to let him get his rest. Since the killings were on television, the world had concerns about knowing a killer was out on the loose. They would become more cautious. The police warned everyone to not be out alone walking the streets, especially at night. Tim didn't want to raise suspicion in any way, so he would keep himself on the low. He took off work for the next few weeks. His mother was happy, but Tim wasn't. The last thing he wanted to do was be home.

"Why are you not working?" His mother asked.
"Jobs are slow right now. It will pick back up in a couple weeks." Tim replied.

His mother wasn't sure that he was being honest, but she liked the idea of him being off work.

"So, I will get to spend more time with you." She stated.

Tim had regretted telling her.

"I still have things to do around here. I will need some space to work on things." Tim responded.

6

When Tim eventually went back to work, he completed his jobs and came home immediately. This was the way he did things for a while. As time continued, Tim looked into taking jobs farther away. He thought if he could be out of his norm, it would give the talk about the killings more time to fade. The company he worked for had signed a new contract with partners overseas. Tim thought this would be a great opportunity for him. He would be gone two months at a time though. This would not make his mother happy in any way.

His mother was feeling better. Tim thought she could handle herself while he was gone, and it would give them more space to apart to work through their problems. After talking to his work place, Tim was set to take his first job out of the country. He grew excited, but still had to tell his mother. One night at dinner, he brought it up in conversation.

"I have another job to attend." Tim said.
"That's great." His mother responded.

A few moments later,

"It's out of the states." He said softly.
"What?" She asked.

His mother glanced up at him.

"You heard me." He said.
"Why would they send you there?" She asked.
Tim sighed.
"I asked them for it." He replied.
"Why would you do that?" She asked.

As usual, she wasn't happy hearing this.

"It's a good opportunity." Tim said.
"I don't like the idea of you leaving the states." She said.

Being tired of his mother's comments, Tim reminded her he wasn't a child anymore.

"I'm a grown man." He said.
"I know, but I still worry." She said.

He didn't know why his mother always questioned everything he did in life. She worried too much he thought.

"I will be fine." He said.
"How long will you be gone?" His mother asked.
"Two months." He replied.

Tim's mom dropped her head and sighed.

"What do you expect me to do if you leave that long?" She asked sadly.
"You have your sister. You will be fine." He replied.

She worried in the moment.

"I want you around more." She said.
"Well, I can't. I have to work." He said.

Not giving up, his mother tried to convince her son to stay. All she wanted was more time with him.

"There are plenty of jobs around here. Take a local one." She suggested.
"I already took the job. I leave tomorrow." Tim said.

His mom was shocked to hear this.

"Tomorrow! And I'm just now hearing about this?" She asked angrily.
"I don't need your approval. I only wanted to let you know." He replied.

She left the table in silence. After cleaning everything up, his mother went home. She knew it didn't matter anymore what she said, Tim would live his life the way he wanted. She would continue to worry about him no matter how old he was. In her eyes, Tim was her baby boy.

The next day, Tim left the States. This felt like a new beginning for him. He hadn't killed for a while and it took everything he had in him to control the urges at times. In a way, he felt a little guilty if he thought back on the women he murdered. *Was Tim regretting what he had done?*

While in the new environment, Tim began dating here and there. Some relationships worked out and some didn't. It never bothered him much. He was content for the first time in a long time. Killing hadn't been on his mind since he left home. He didn't want to go back to hurting women. *Would Tim find a way to keep himself from killing another innocent woman?*

After a few weeks, women started rejecting dates with him. Word on the streets traveled fast about Tim not being very compatible. This began to bother him after a while of hearing others talk.

"Why can't I find someone nice?" Tim thought.

He questioned himself a lot when it came to women. Not understanding what was wrong with him, Tim lost more self-confidence in the dating world. He would eventually give up on the thought that he deserved a life partner. Trying to go out with women faded over time. The constant rejection became too much on him, so dating didn't last long while he was out of the

States at work. *What would he do with himself now?* Tim received a phone call from his mother one night. He was hesitant, but finally picked up the call. He wondered what she wanted.

> *"I haven't heard from you since you left."* His mother said.
> *"I've been busy."* Tim said.
> *"Do you like it there?"* She asked.

Being patient with his mother, Tim answered her questions.

> *"It's no different than back home."* He replied.
> *"Have you met any friends?"* She asked.
> *"Not really."* Tim replied.

She paused for moment.

> *"When are you going to start dating again?"* His mother asked.
> *"That's none of your business."* He said.
> *"I just want you to be happy."* She said.

This made Tim upset.

> *"Please, stay out of my life problems."* Tim said as he hung the phone up.

He had no interest in discussing his love life with his mother. In his mind, she needed to leave him alone about it. Tim only had a couple more weeks before returning home. Avoiding any more calls from his mother, he was sure she would continue prying into his business once he was home.

> *"I wish she would stop bothering me."* Tim thought.

On his way back to his room one night after work, he was thinking about all the rejection from women he had received. A woman approached him asking for directions. Tim stood for a moment admiring her. She was talking, but he didn't hear it. After a few minutes, the woman stared at him strangely. This is when Tim came back to his senses. He was confused.

"I'm sorry, what?" Tim asked.
"Didn't you hear anything I just said?" She asked in confusion.

Tim glanced at the woman.

"Are you alright?" The woman asked.
"Yes, sorry, I was just in deep thought." Tim replied.
"Do you want to grab a drink and talk about it?" She asked.

Tim wasn't sure if that was a good idea or not.

"Maybe I shouldn't." Tim replied.

The woman was alone. Tim had wondered about her.

"Where are you from?" Tim asked.
"I'm from the states. I was looking for directions." She replied.
"I'm not from around here either. I wouldn't be much help to you." Tim explained.

They glanced at each other once more.

"Are you from the states too?" She asked.
"Yes." Tim replied.

After a few moments,

"I'm supposed to go meet some friends at a club. Do you want to come?" She asked.
"Maybe some other time." Tim replied.
"Okay." She responded nicely.

The woman walked away. As she got down the street, Tim decided to follow her. Something about her was attractive. She eventually found the club. Tim walked close until she exited an hour later with a friend. The two friends laughed and talked as they walked the streets.

"I had a great time tonight." The woman said.
"Me too!" The friend said excitedly.

After a while, the two friends parted ways. Tim continued to follow the woman down a dark biking path in the park. There were tall trees all around. Tim hadn't checked out this part of town since he arrived. Suddenly, she stopped to tie her shoes. While she was knelt on the ground, Tim went in for the choke. She fell out. Tim was satisfied he had overpowered her.

"This is going to be an easy kill." Thought Tim.

He dragged the woman under a tree. After ripping her clothes off, he quickly posed her body for a picture.

"Finally, I get another picture to add to my graveyard collection at home." Tim whispered to himself as he took the photo.

As the woman began to wake up,

"Where am I?" She whispered.

She glanced up to see Tim standing in front of her.

"You. You're the guy from earlier." She said.

Tim stood silently for a few short seconds. Then, he knelt beside her. At first, he didn't say anything.

"Why are you doing this to me?" The woman asked.
"Someone has to pay for my heartbreak." Tim replied.

At that moment, Tim strangled the woman until she gasped for her last breath. He was satisfied with this killing. Leaving into the darkness, Tim went back to his room to think.

"Now, I need to go back to the states." Tim said to himself.

Tim loaded the plane with his things to head home. In the middle of the flight, the plane landed.

"This is not my destination." He thought.

He wondered what was going on. *Had Tim boarded the wrong flight?* After some investigation, the plane was having mechanical issues. Everyone would be delayed overnight at the airport. This didn't make Tim happy to hear. He decided to get a room at the airport hotel until the next morning. As he was waiting on the desk clerk, a woman behind him made conversation.

"Are you a photographer?" She asked.

Tim looked down to see he still had his camera around his neck. It was obvious what he did for a living.

"Yes." He replied.
"What kind of photography do you do?" She asked.
"I travel to different events." Tim replied.
"Interesting." The woman said.

About that time, the clerk entered the room to assist them. After checking in, Tim went to his room to rest. It was a little loud at the hotel with the bar down the hall. Later, Tim went for a walk. The noise was keeping him awake. As he exited the room, the woman he had seen earlier was passing by.

"Hey, do you want to go have a drink with me?" She asked.

Tim was tempted but knew he needed to keep a low profile.

"Maybe next time." He replied.

He left the hotel alone. It was dark and getting late. A while later, Tim headed back toward the hotel. Not many people were on the streets. Most of them were at bars having fun with others. Close to the hotel, Tim observed the woman walking around drunk as if she didn't know where she was. His urge to kill grew strong as he watched her. He talked himself into killing her.

"She will never know what happened to her." Tim thought.

With the urges even stronger, Tim decided to end her life. This would be another easy one for him.

"Hey." Tim hollered.

The woman looked across the lot. She recognized Tim and stumbled over to him slowly.

"You are that guy from the front desk earlier." She said as she walked toward him.

Tim thought for a moment.

"Maybe she's not as drunk as I thought." Tim whispered to himself.

The woman stumbled.

"Are you Okay?" Tim asked.
"Yes, I just need to walk it off." She replied.

After a few seconds,

"Well, you can walk with me." Tim suggested.
"Where are we going?" She asked.

Tim thought fast.

"For a walk around town." He replied.
"Okay." She giggled.

They walked into the darkness together. Eventually, the two ended up around the back of the building. Tim thought this would be the opportunity he needed to kill her. She was drunk and weak. So, it would be easy for him.

Grabbing her around the neck, he strangled her. Not putting her to sleep like the others, but killing her. The woman had been drinking and stopped breathing when Tim tried to choke her out. He dragged her body toward the dumpster behind the hotel.

"She's dead already." He said disappointed.

Tim quickly took a picture before throwing her body into the dumpster. He didn't bother ripping her clothes off since she had died. Liking to pose women naked and taking a picture as they awake, Tim wasn't interested in finishing his usual routine.

The next morning, the Police wanted to watch the video camera on the hotel but found that the cameras were not working properly. Tim was lucky that night. Getting onto the plane, he went home to bury his new photos.

7

Tim didn't waste any time developing his pictures. He admired his killings for a while before hiking to his victim's graveyard. There, he would bury them next to the others. After burying, he stayed longer to relax with nature. Losing track of time, Tim didn't realize how late into the afternoon it had become. His stomach growling, he decided to go back to the house. On the way, Tim noticed something. Toward the entrance of the trail, he saw a ring lying on the ground. It was an expensive ring. He wondered who's it could be. Picking it up, he heard a voice.

"Thank God you found my ring! I have been looking everywhere for it. Give it to me."

Tim glanced over to see his cousin.

"What are you doing here?" He asked.
"I came to see everyone." She replied.
"Why is your ring on my trail?" Tim asked.
"Your trail?" She asked.
"Yes." He replied.

His cousin stared with confusion.

"I wasn't aware it was your trail." His cousin said.
"It's on my property." He stated.
"I didn't go far. Just right here observing the trees. I like being in nature just like my father." She said.

He began to be rude towards her.

"You shouldn't be out here at all." He said.
"Well, sorry." She said.
"Don't make it a habit." He said.

He was relieved to hear that she didn't make it back to his graveyard area. Giving the ring back to her, Tim walked her into the house. There, his mother and aunt were also. Tim looked confused.

"I guess I missed the invitation." Tim stated.
"We are family. You should be happy to see us." His Aunt said.

He wasn't happy to see unexpected visitors.

"Why were you out there so long?" His Aunt asked.

Tim thought his aunt was intruding on his business too much.

"I like the woods and nature. It evidently runs in the family. Leave me alone." Tim said sarcastically.

His Aunt jumped into the conversation. She couldn't stand to hear Tim disrespect his mother in front of her.

"Why do you treat your mother that way?" She asked.

Tim glanced at his aunt angrily.

"My relationship with my mother is none of your business." He said.
"Tim, stop." His cousin said.

He looked around at everyone staring at him. At that moment, things appeared awkward.

"You know what, everyone go home." Tim said.

Without another word spoken, everyone left. Tim didn't want to waste time arguing with his family. Not caring what others had to say, he focused on work and other things. Lying in bed, Tim thought about Ava. He decided to take his next job near the town she lived in.

"If I see her, it will make my life better." He thought.

Early the next morning, Tim packed for his trip. He couldn't wait to leave town. His family was annoying him and he needed to get away from them. After loading the car, his aunt approached him once more.

"Your mother cried last night." She said.

Tim stood in silence next to his car.

"Why do you upset her like that?" She asked.

He rolled his eyes to his aunt.

"She gets herself upset." He replied.
"You talk to her terrible." His aunt said.

He began to grow angry again. He thought if maybe she knew the truth, she would leave him alone.

"Do you even know what happened?" Tim asked.

Out of curiosity, she had to ask.

"What do you mean?" She asked curiously.
"Oh, so she hid it from you too." He replied.

Now he had his aunt's attention. She was the type to want to know everyone's business.

"Hid what?" She asked.
"She didn't tell you that my father wasn't my real father?" Tim asked.

His aunt was even more confused. To her, Tim wasn't making a lot of sense. She wanted him to say what he had to say.

"Now you are talking nonsense." She said.
"No, it's true. Ask her." He responded.

Both stared at each other for a few short seconds. His aunt debated whether to believe him.

"She would have told me if it were true. We didn't keep secrets." She said.
"Well, she kept this one from you." Tim said sarcastically.

Being sure that Tim was lying, she wanted him to explain.

"Tell me about it." She said.
"I'm sure she will tell you the story now that it's out in the open. Go ask her." He said.

His aunt walked away as Tim left in his car. He was sure she would understand once she knew the truth about the secret his mother kept. Once at his destination, he checked into his hotel as usual and ventured off onto the streets. It was a nice city town he thought. Standing by the waters next to a walking path, a voice from behind caught his attention.

"I can't believe you're here." The voice said.

Tim turned around to see Ava with a big belly. It looked as if she were ready to have a baby.

"Wow, I guess it worked out with your ex?" He asked.
"No, actually didn't." She replied.

Tim was surprised at the moment. He never imagined that she would move on so quickly from her ex.

"So, he got you pregnant and left?" Tim asked.
"Not quite." She replied softly.

Tim wondered where the baby had come from. He thought maybe she had met up with a random guy.

"I thought about it after you walked away, and I knew it would be a mistake if I went back to him, but by that time, you were gone." She explained.

At that moment, he was trying to figure out what she was saying. *What did she want him to know?*

"Who's baby?" He asked.
"It's your baby." She replied.
"Mine?" He asked in shock.
"Yes, your baby." She replied.

Tim wasn't sure what to say. He never knew she was pregnant or he wouldn't have left.

"I'm sorry, I didn't know you were..." Tim tried to apologize.
"It's okay. You didn't know." She said.

The conversation suddenly got interrupted.

"Hey, babe! Sorry I'm late. Work has been busy." A man said.

Tim looked at him wondering who he was. He had thought maybe Ava wanted him back at first.

"Um, this is Tim. My baby's dad." Ava said as she introduced her man to Tim.

The man tried to shake Tim's hand but that wasn't what Tim wanted to do. He stood in silence staring at the new man.

"What's this?" Tim asked.
"I'm sorry, I never thought I would see you again. I eventually just stopped looking." She replied.

The new guy began feeling awkward. He wanted to give them some privacy to talk things through.

"You two talk and I will see you later on tonight. Just call me." The man said as he walked away.
"Get rid of the baby and move on." Tim said.

She was in disbelief.

"That's crazy. I'm not getting rid of my baby." She said.
"It doesn't need my blood anyway." Tim said.

Ava couldn't believe what Tim was saying. *How could Tim ask Ava to do such a thing?*

"What do you mean?" She asked.
"Trust me when I say that." He said.

Both argued about the subject a few minutes longer. Tim begged her just to get rid of it. He didn't want a child having his blood and living with the urges of killing like he has his whole life. Eventually, Ava left not wanting to hear what Tim had to say. She was willing to raise the baby herself if she had to. Angry, Tim went back to his hotel room for the night. He couldn't handle the thought of bringing another child into the world that carried the killer genes.

Wanting to tell her the real reason, he was scared that it would expose him too much. He wasn't ready to go to prison any time soon. *Was Tim being like his mother?* He realized how the secret his mother kept made him feel. After some time to think about it, the decision was made to tell Ava the truth. Only then would she understand and decide to end the pregnancy before it was too late.

"I have to tell her the truth no matter what happens to me." Tim whispered to himself.

The next morning, Tim was determined to find Ava and tell her everything. The only problem was, he couldn't find her. He walked the whole town looking, but came to dead ends with his search.

"Maybe she went back to her town." He thought.

Tim risked going back to her old apartment. When he knocked at the door, an old man answered.

"Can I help you?" The old man asked.

He stood there for a moment.

"I'm looking for Ava." Tim replied.
"She moved out of town." The old man said.

Walking away disappointed, Tim had to figure out where Ava was. He left back to his work area quickly before being recognized. Another search of the city the next day ended with no leads to her whereabouts. He went on to his job. Later, he lay in bed discouraged with life. He had to find her. All of a sudden, he received a phone call from his mother.

"Hello." Tim said as he answered the phone.
"Why did you tell my sister?" His mother asked.

Tim grew angry quickly. His mother should be more worried about why she kept the secret.

"This is nobody's fault but yours. If you would have been honest from the beginning then we wouldn't be having this issue right now." Tim replied.

She sighed with sadness.

"It's not my fault the agency switched the sperm." She explained.
"You have no idea what that secret could have saved in this world, if only I would have known." Tim said.

Tim's mother became confused and worried. She didn't like the way Tim was talking at the moment.

"What are you talking about?" She asked.

Tim sat in silence. He wanted to tell her what was going on so she could see what his life was like, but he hesitated.

"Tim?" His mother responded trying to get him to answer.
"Just forget about it now. The damage has already been done. You will find out one day." Tim said.

She wasn't giving up.

"Tim, you are worrying me. Please, talk to me." She pleaded.

After a few long seconds, Tim threw a question to her. He wanted to know how much she paid attention to him in his younger days.

"Did you see me as an odd kid?" Tim asked.
"I never looked at you as odd. You appeared normal to me. Just a little quiet." She replied.

He figured she never paid attention.

"Well, I wasn't normal." Tim said.
"What do you mean?" She asked.

Tim thought for a few minutes. It seemed to him that his mother worried more about herself.

"Didn't you worry at all about how the secret you were keeping would affect me as an adult?" Tim asked.
"At the time I thought it be best for you not to know. Maybe I was wrong to do that." She replied.

Not wanting to say another word, Tim hung the phone up. His mother didn't know he was a killer. He wanted to complete his work and get out of the city he was in. Knowing he could never have a normal relationship with his mother, Tim tried to focus more on his jobs.

8

Still thinking about his soon-to-be baby, Tim grew frustrated that he hadn't seen Ava again. He wanted her to realize what she was going to bring in to life. The last night at the hotel, Tim had just come in that evening. He noticed a cleaning lady in one of the rooms he passed. The door was propped open while she was changing bed linens. Tim thought this was an opportunity.

"Isn't it late to be cleaning rooms?" Tim thought.

He turned around going back toward the room. As he stood outside the doorway, the lady glanced at him.

"Can I help you?" She asked.

Tim had to come up with something to say. The maid was getting suspicious of him staring at her.

"Um, do you have any clean towels?" He asked quickly.
"Yes." The lady replied as she walked to her cart to give Tim clean towels.

The moment was awkward as she handed Tim the towels. She appeared cautious of him.

"Here you go." She said.
"Thanks." Tim said as he continued to stare her down.

Tim glanced around the hallway but didn't see anyone. Suddenly, he pushed the cleaning cart into the room and shut the door. The maid turned quickly as she grew nervous about his actions.

"What are you doing?" The lady asked.

Tim stood in silence.

"You need to get out of here." She said.

With Tim still standing in silence, she tried to leave the room, but he wouldn't let her.

"HELP!" She shouted.

The lady tried to fight Tim but he overpowered her. All of a sudden, she fell to the floor. Tim had accidentally snapped her neck during the struggle. This angered him. He grabbed her lifeless body and threw her to the bed. Then, he stripped her clothes off and posed her body for a quick picture. This would be the first time he took a photo of a dead woman.

He ran out of the room and down the hallway to his room for the night. He had hoped that no one saw him. Checking out early the next morning, Tim didn't want to stay around. Before he could drive away, Tim was stopped and questioned by a police officer outside the hotel.

"Do you know anything about the maid killing last night?" The cop asked.
"No, I don't." Tim replied.

He knew to act as normal as possible.

"You didn't see or hear anything?" The cop asked.
"No, I didn't." Tim replied.

Tim began to get nervous.

"I need to run your name through our system before you leave." The cop said.

Tim waited anxiously while the police officer checked his name. Eventually, he finally returned.

"One last thing, can we check your car?" The cop asked.

This concerned Tim.

"For what?" Tim asked.
"Just a routine we are doing with everyone that stayed at the hotel last night." The cop explained.
"Sure." Tim said as he stepped out of the car.

Waiting outside the car, Tim watched as the police searched his things. He didn't take anything from the victim, so there was nothing to find. Their actions still made him anxious.

"Is this your camera?" The police asked.
"Yes, I'm a photographer." Tim replied.

Tim was on edge as the officer continued to question him.

"Do you travel a lot?" The police asked.
"Yes, my job requires it." Tim replied.

For some reason, Tim thought the police were suspicious of him. As they finished searching, another officer approached the car. The two officers made conversation with each other.

"We reviewed the video camera attached in that hallway." The officer said to another.
"Did it show anything?" The officer next to Tim asked.

Tim listened closely as they continued.

"It was not working correctly. There was a part you could see a little but it was blurry and out of focus. We could see a guy in some kind of a hooded sweatshirt running out of the room, but it wasn't clear." The approaching officer explained.

"Take it to the station. We will have forensics try to get a better picture." The officer next to Tim said.

The police looked at Tim. At first, he didn't know what to say. After a long moment, the officer spoke.

"We will be staying in touch. You are free to leave now." The officer said.

Tim went home concerned that the police thought it was him. Even though they couldn't prove it completely, it still made Tim nervous. He thought maybe his killing days should be over.

"Why do you seem anxious?" Tim's mother asked.

He turned around fast to see his mother standing at the doorway of his bedroom upstairs.

"Why are you sneaking up on me?" Tim asked angrily.
"I just came to visit." She replied.
"Did you knock?" Tim asked.

His mother looked confused.

"I'm your mom. I didn't know I was required to knock." She replied.
"Well, you should." Tim said.

She didn't like the way he had been treating her lately. To her, the secret she kept wasn't such a big deal.

"When is this going to stop?" His mother asked.

"What are you talking about?" Tim asked.
"The way you have been treating me." She replied.

Tim stayed quiet.

"Okay, are you going to tell me why you were so anxious when I walked in?" She asked.
"Don't worry about it." He replied.
"If you are in trouble, let me help." She said.

He glanced over to his mother. He wondered for a moment if she was beginning to suspect him also.

"What makes you think I'm in trouble?" Tim asked.
"The way you were acting was strange." She replied.

Tim walked out of the room with his mother quickly following. She was known to pry into Tim's business.

"Where are you going?" She asked.
"I have work to do. You can show yourself out." Tim replied.

Needing to develop his pictures, Tim went to the basement. His mother knew she couldn't follow him. This was an area he allowed no one to enter. He had hoped his mother would leave before he was finished. Later that evening, he returned upstairs. He poked his head around the corner to look around.

"Good, she is gone." He whispered to himself.

With his mother not around, Tim left through the woods to visit his victim's graveyard. He had to bury his new treasure before anyone saw it. While there, he spent time reflecting on life. Tim wondered if he should move his treasures out into the wilderness farther so the police wouldn't find them one day. When darkness fell, Tim made his way back to the house.

Eventually, he sat to book his next job. As he thought about it, Tim changed his mind. He wanted to take another trip somewhere in the wilderness away from life. This would give him time away from home also. Instead of booking a job, he paid for a vacation. The following day, Tim packed his things and left. Surprisingly, his mother never showed up to interrupt.

Enjoying his trip, Tim didn't worry about anything. He stayed at a cabin by a lake. It was a small place secluded away from society. Something Tim needed at the time. His days were spent on the lake boating and in the woods hiking. At night, he spent his time lying under the stars. Everything was great until he received a phone call from his mother again.

"What is it now?" Tim asked.
"How many more days will you be working?" His mother asked.
"I'm not working." Tim replied.

His mother was confused.

"You are not home. I thought you were at work." She said.
"I'm on vacation. I will be home in a few more days." Tim said.

He hung the phone up.

"That conversation didn't go as bad as I thought it would." Tim thought.

There was no killing on this trip. Tim honestly enjoyed his time alone. This was a change for him. Now, he had to return home to pick up another job. As he pulled up to his house, Tim noticed something odd. The front door was open. Tim remembered shutting his door before he left.

"I bet my mother didn't shut it all the way." He whispered.

Tim carried his stuff into the house. Suddenly, he heard a noise in the kitchen. He hesitantly went to observe.

"Is someone in my house?" He asked.

There was no answer.

"Hello." Tim said as he moved closer.

Once he turned the corner to go into the kitchen area,

"Surprise!"

Tim couldn't believe his eyes. A few family members were standing in front of him with his mother. He hadn't seen them in a long time. Tim wondered why his mother would bring them to his house.

"What is going on?" Tim asked.
"Did you forget that it was your birthday?" His mother asked.

Tim thought for a moment. With his life being so busy, he was lucky to keep up with anything outside his work and killings.

"I guess I did." He replied.
"Well, you knew your mother wasn't going to forget." His aunt said.

He looked over at the table behind everyone. There was a lot of food and a big cake. He was surprised anyone even acknowledged him for his birthday. Usually, he spent it alone.

"*Let's eat!*" His cousin Ray said.

They all ate and had cake together. Tim was quiet during the party. Ray had wondered why.

"*Let's go for a walk birthday boy.*" Ray said.

The two began walking out back of the house. Tim wondered what he would want to talk about.

"*How have you been?*" Ray asked.
"*I've been fine.*" Tim replied.

They continued walking.

"*Your mom says different.*" Ray said.
"*She's always worrying.*" Tim said.

Ray looked over at Tim.

"*Aren't that what mothers do?*" Ray asked.

Tim stopped to stare at Ray.

"*Did you come to lecture me?*" Tim asked.

Ray shrugged his shoulders at Tim.

"*No, just want to make sure you are okay.*" Ray replied.
"*I will tell you like I tell my mother. I am fine.*" Tim said.
"*Okay, calm down.*" Ray said.

Tim glanced around. He wasn't paying attention to how far they had walked. Being able to see his victim's graveyard ahead, Tim needed to get Ray out of the woods quickly. This made him nervous to have someone so close to his treasures. *What would Ray say if he knew what Tim had done?*

"Hey, Let's head back to the house." Tim suggested.
"You don't want to keep walking?" Ray asked.
"No." Tim replied quickly.

Ray noticed a change in Tim's actions.

"Why are you so anxious all of a sudden?" Ray asked.

He had to make an excuse to lower suspicion.

"It's getting dark. I want to head back." Tim replied.
"I didn't know you were afraid of the dark." Ray said.

Tim began to get discouraged. He didn't want to kill his cousin. He needed to get him out of the woods.

"I'm not. I just want to get back to the house." Tim said.

A few seconds later,

"Fine." Ray said.
"Let's go." Tim said.

Ray Proceeded to go first, but he was still suspicious of Tim. They returned to the house together for the rest of the party. Tim wanted to relax. After everyone left, he cleaned up and went to bed.

9

Tim was fully relaxed from the trip he had just got back from. Also, he didn't have urges to kill while gone. Then again, he was isolated. The party was nice, but he had wished his mother would have consulted him about it first. Not being fond of her running his life, he still pretended to be thankful.

Choosing to try another job out of the States again, he would be in a different area this time. He would work on controlling himself from killing. Knowing he could keep it together to a point, Tim would avoid it the best he could. *Could Tim accomplish the goal of not killing?*

His mother wasn't happy either. She hated it when Tim was far away and gone too long. Although, Tim really didn't care. No matter what his mother had said and done, he did what he wanted in life. Nothing would change that in his mind. Having another day until he left, time was spent packing and loading. His mother made sure she didn't miss seeing him before he left.

"Where are you going this time?" She asked.
"Out of the states again." Tim replied.

She was mad when he told her this.

"You know I don't like you being that far away." She said.
"It's for my job." He said.

His mother began to make suggestions to give him better ideas.

"You could get a factory job around here." She suggested.
"I like to travel." He said.

His mother seemed discouraged.

"You are my life. I don't want something happening to you." She said.

"You have other family. And besides, nothing is going to happen to me." Tim said.

"You don't know that." She said.

"Of course I do." He said.

She wasn't convinced.

"I'm a big boy now. Stop worrying." He said.

As much as his mother tried, she couldn't change his mind on anything. He was stubborn in her eyes. She had no choice but to accept what he wanted to do. His mother had hoped that one day things would get better between them and he would choose to spend more time at home with her. Knowing some of it had to do with the secret she kept from him his whole life, she couldn't change what already was. Tim needed to find a way to forgive her and put the past behind him. Holding a grudge wasn't good for him. She wanted nothing more than to fix the damage that it had caused him inside. Although, she had no idea just how much damage it had really caused. The real question was, *could it be changed?*

Once at his destination, Tim settled in. Being there for a couple of weeks, he wanted to see what the area had to offer. It was awkward for him. Everyone dressed differently than he was used to. This made him stand out a little more than others. Tim didn't like people noticing him. Deciding to buy some of their clothing, he thought this would make him fit in with the crowd.

The streets were full of tables set up for merchandise to sell. It almost reminded him of a flea market. Happy people flooded the town. He wasn't sure how he would do in a place like this. While looking at some of the things people were selling, a man approached him.

"I see you are not from around here." The man said.
"No." Tim said.

Tim wasn't sure what to say.

"Where are you from?" The man asked.
"The states." Tim replied.

A few minutes later,

"What brings you here?" The man asked.
"Work." Tim replied.

Tim noticed the man staring at him. This didn't make Tim comfortable at all. The man noticed Tim acting strangely.

"I see the camera you have around your neck." The man said.
"Yes." Tim said.
"Are you a journalist?" The man asked.

Shaking his head, he answered calmly.

"I'm a photographer." Tim replied.
"Some journalists have traveled through here with cameras too." The man explained.
"Well, I'm not a journalist." Tim said.

Tim walked around to the other side of the table with the man following. He held his composure.

"Are you here for the concert event?" The man asked.
"Yes, I was hired to do pictures for the band." Tim replied.

The man appeared more settle at this point.

"I will be there too." The man said.
"Nice." Tim said.

Tim began to walk away.

"How long will you be in town?" The man asked.
"A couple of weeks. I'm doing the band job in a few days and then next week I'm doing a job over in the next town." Tim explained.
"Maybe we will see each other again." The man said.
"Maybe." Tim said as he walked away.

Tim wasn't sure if the man worked for the police or not, but he wanted the man to know he had a good reason to be in the area. He didn't want anyone to be suspicious of him being there. Tim walked away from the man in a hurry. He grabbed food and went to his room for the night.

A few days later, he attended the concert for photos. There was a big crowd that attended. People were arm to arm trying to walk around. Drinking was a big thing that night. Tim had a spot in front of the stage so he could get good pictures of the band. It was loud and everyone was rowdy.

By the time the band had stopped playing, Tim was more than ready to leave. He began feeling overwhelmed with so many around him. Space was needed along with some quiet time. The band wrapped up and the drunk crowd started making their way out. Tim stayed on the side until mostly everyone had gone.

"Now I can finally leave." Tim thought to himself.

Outside the concert area, Tim noticed a drunk woman. He decided to approach her carefully.

"Are you okay?" Tim asked.

The woman seemed confused.

"I'm trying to find my friends." The woman slurred.
"I will help you find them." Tim offered.
"You will?" She asked.
"Come with me." Tim said.

The woman agreed and walked with Tim into the darkness, never to be seen again. The next few days, there was a search for the woman, but no leads. She was reported missing by her friends. There had been a lot of people at the concert and mostly everyone was drunk, so no one noticed when the woman went missing or what even happened to her. *Did Tim know?* He wouldn't tell. If Tim did do something to her, he knew how to dispose of a body and evidence. Nothing would be traced back to him.

Tim moved on to the next job. Trying to focus more on his work, he never thought about the disappearing woman. His mother called to check on him, but he told her he was busy and couldn't talk. He had one goal in mind at that point, get his work done and go back to the States. *Did Tim kill the missing woman?* He was the last known person to see her and he had a history of killing. But, that didn't prove he did anything wrong this time around.

Eventually finishing his time there, he traveled home quietly. Once at home, Tim carried his things inside. He wanted to hurry and develop his photos. *What would make him so anxious?* As he approached the basement door, he heard a sound. Slowly going down the steps, Tim continued hearing noises.

"What is that?" He thought.

He looked over and couldn't believe what he was seeing. His mother was searching through his stuff.

"What are you doing?" Tim said angrily.

His mother turned around quickly to see her son standing across the room watching her.

"I didn't know you were home." His mother said nervously.
"Why are searching through my stuff?" Tim asked.
"I was just curious about your work." She replied.

Tim was mad at his mother for sneaking into the basement. This was an invasion of his privacy.

"You are not supposed to be down here." Tim said.
"I'm sorry." His mother claimed.
"Go home. I have work to finish." Tim said as he walked past his mother.

His mother left quietly. She didn't want to upset Tim more than he was. Feeling bad about going through his things, his mother wanted to make it up to him somehow so he wouldn't be mad. Tim was happy she was gone. Now, he could work on developing his photos. There was one photo in particular that he couldn't wait to see. *What was it?* Soon, Tim would be happy to see it finished.

He held the photo high to observe. *What was it a photo of?* It was a picture of the missing woman from the concert night.

"Yeah, I killed her." He whispered.

Tim sighed with great relief and satisfaction. He thought back to that night. The woman walked off into the darkness with Tim. They ended up on a beach next to the ocean. She tried to kiss Tim but he wasn't interested. He felt overwhelmed by the concert and needed relief. He strangled her to death, taking a photo of her lifeless body on the sand. The second time he had ever taken a picture of a dead woman with clothes on. *Would this be the new norm?*

The easiest thing to do at the moment was to bury her in the sand. Tim pulled her body off to the side of the beach while he dug a hole. Not a normal hole, but deeper than a grave would be so no one would ever find her. Now, he needed to bury his treasure. Walking out the door, he ran into his mother.

"I thought I told you to go home?" Tim asked.
"I wanted to come cook for you. I'm sorry about earlier. Please eat with me." His mother replied.
"I'm not hungry. I'm going for a walk." Tim said.

He walked towards the woods as his mother followed closely behind. Tim didn't like this.

"Let me go with you. It would be great to spend time with you. We can eat when we get back." His mother pleaded.

Tim grew angry as he turned to face his mother. He wanted his mother to leave him alone.

"No!" Tim said loudly.

In fear, she backed away from Tim.

"Why not?" She asked.
"I want to be by myself for a while." He replied.

He continued to walk into the woods.

"Fine. I'll wait for you here and cook when you return." She stated.
"Go home! I'll be fine tonight. I told you I wasn't hungry. I ate earlier." He said angrily.

Finally, she left. Tim could go to his victim's graveyard to bury his new treasure. He glanced around carefully to make sure no one was following him. With his mother being so nosy lately, he took precautions. *Would someone find his graveyard one day?* Tim had to think clearly with every step he took in life. He had been careless a few times now, risking being caught. There was no room for mistakes anymore. From now on, he would be smarter with his killings.

After venturing back to the house, Tim booked another job. Wanting to keep an eye on his mother, he took a job closer to home. This was not his norm when it came to her. Usually, he tried to travel far to avoid her. Resting in bed, he thought about Ava wondering if his child had been born yet.

"She had to have had it by now." He thought.

Tim wasn't sure if he would ever see Ava again and get to meet his child. One thing he was sure of, the child had killer blood in it. The next morning, he loaded his car to leave.

"Are you leaving the States again?" His mother asked.

Tim wasn't surprised to see her there. She made it a habit to stop by knowing he was leaving.

"No. I will be back in a few days." Tim replied.
"Good." She said.

He glanced over at his mother while she was still standing there as he was ready to drive off.

"Stay out of my house while I'm gone this time." Tim said as he pulled away.
"If that's what you want." She said.

Again, Tim settled in once he arrived at his job site. After two days, he completed his job and was ready to leave the next morning. He decided to get food and go back to his room for the night when a woman accidentally ran into him while he was walking. He gazed at her.

"Watch where you are going freak!" She hollered at him.

He was a little confused as to why she blamed him.

"Excuse me?" Tim asked.
"You heard me!" She replied.

Being discouraged, Tim was rude back.

"You ran into me." Tim said.
"No, you ran into me." The woman said as she walked off.
"Whatever you say." Tim said.

Tim grew angry. It was the woman's fault for running into him. He followed her silently down the street. She didn't notice. Darkness had fallen and not too many people were out walking.

"I will show her a freak." Tim whispered to himself.

As soon as she hit an alley, Tim went in for the kill. Again, he would use strangling to death as the kill. This time, he was harsher because of her rudeness against him earlier. While she was gasping, he made her stare into his eyes. Tim wanted her to see how evil he was.

"You shouldn't call others freaks! Now, you have to die." He whispered loudly into her face.

Looking into his eyes as she took her last breath, she knew it was over. One mistake with the wrong person had cost her life.

Tim ran off into the darkness after the killing. He didn't want a picture of her.

Getting up the next morning as if nothing happened, Tim returned home and life was back to normal. There were no signs that his mother had been in his house while he was gone. This made Tim content.

"Finally, I can relax." Tim said to himself.

10

Things began to get heated again over all the killings. The news covered the story heavily. Everyone walked around talking about it. No one wanted to be alone on the streets. People started hanging out in groups. Everybody was a suspect. Tim decided to stay home for a while. He had the funds to do so. Tim told his work he had become ill and was taking some time off. His mother became curious over time. One evening over dinner, she would try to figure out what was going on.

"Why haven't you been working?" She asked.
"I took some time off." He replied.

Of course, he knew his mother wouldn't't let it go.

"Why?" She asked.
"I just wanted to take a break from traveling." Tim replied.

Tim continued to eat. He didn't want to talk, but he knew his mother would continue asking questions.

"Are you going to get another job?" His mother asked.
"No, I'm keeping the job I have." He replied.

His mother was still suspicious. She could tell that Tim was hiding something from her.

"This isn't like you." She said.
"What do you mean?" He asked.
"Taking off work like this." She replied.

He tried to be convincing.

"It's just for a bit." He said.
"But, you never takes breaks." She said.

He tried to maintain his calmness.

"It's not a big deal." He said.
"You never stay home. Tell me the real reason you are not working." She said.

Tim was growing agitated by all the questioning his mother was doing. He eventually spoke up.

"Why do you question everything I do?" Tim asked.
"I worry about you." His mother replied.
"Well, don't." He said.
"I will always worry." She said.
"You don't need to." He said.

All he wanted to do was finish his dinner in peace without his mother aggravating him.

"Are you in some kind of trouble?" She asked.

Tim glanced at his mother angrily. He had enough of her worrying about him so much.

"No!" Tim said loudly.
"Then, why are you not working?" She asked again.

Tim knew he had to come up with something to keep his mother from questioning or she wouldn't stop.

"Look, you have been wanting me to stay home more, so I talked to my work and they let me have some time off." Tim replied.

This made his mom happy for a minute, but she wasn't sure that her son was telling the truth. Tim thought he had his mom convinced that he was trying to work on their relationship. Both finished dinner and parted their ways for the night. His mother would return in the morning for breakfast.

"How did you sleep last night?" His mother asked.
"Good." Tim replied.
"Do you want to hang out today and do something together?" She asked.

This was not what Tim wanted.

"Actually, I have a few things to do today." He replied.
"I thought you wanted to hang out with me more?" She asked.

Tim Made another excuse so he could get time away from her. He needed to be alone.

"My work called and they need me to do a few things for them." He replied.

This confused his mother.

"You are leaving on a job?" She asked.
"No, just some things from home. I can send them what they need from here." He replied.

She decided to leave him alone for a while.

"Okay. I'll check on you later." She said.

Tim wasn't looking forward to seeing her later. Even so, he knew to keep himself from becoming too angry with her. He didn't want her to find out the real reason for taking a work absence. That afternoon, Tim decided to go visit his victim graveyard again. Not to bury this time, but to reflect.

Making his way through the woods, Tim watched to make sure his mother wasn't following. Once to his graveyard, he observed his surroundings. It was a nice day with good weather. The tall trees were swaying slightly with the breeze. The sounds of birds chirping could be heard throughout the woods. Tim loved being in nature.

He knelt beside each grave marking and thought back to the killings one by one. Then, he sat wondering what would happen to him if he were ever caught. Out of nowhere, Tim began to cry. He couldn't handle the thought of being locked up. This was when he thought about ending his life. If he killed himself, Tim wouldn't have to live to face the consequences of what he had done. He started to question his life in general and wondered why things had to be the way they were.

"Why did they have to mix the semen?"

Every few seconds, Tim cried out a question.

"Why did I have to be born?" His existence.
"Why didn't she just tell me the truth, so I could have gotten help?" His lying mother.
"Why was my wife taken?" His wife dying.
"Why does life have to be this way?" And life.

Tim continued to cry out and question life until he fell over on the ground. Gazing toward the sky, Tim fell asleep with tears still running down his face. *Had Tim completely lost his mind at this point?* While sleeping, he began to have a nightmare. In this dream, Tim was being chased by all of his victims. For the first time, Tim felt the fear of his victims. A few minutes later, he sat up screaming. The birds flew away scared as he breathed heavily. His heart raced as he glanced around to figure out where he was. Tim had forgotten he fell asleep at the graveyard.

"I have to go." Tim said to himself.

He quickly ran back to the house for a shower. He was covered in sweat from the nightmare, and dirt from lying on the ground. As he entered the house, his mother came running.

"Where have you been?" She asked.

Tim was in a rush.

"I can't talk right now." Tim replied.

His mother observed the dirt all over her son. She knew something wasn't right with him.

"What's wrong?" She asked.
"Nothing! I'm going to get a shower." Tim hollered.
"Tim?" She questioned.

His mother was concerned about what was going on. She made breakfast while he showered. While eating, Tim thought about Ava again. The truth was, he felt sorry for the child she decided to bring into the world. It would only be another killer. Even if it meant risking his own self, Tim had to find Ava so he could warn her and the child could get help. He thought that was the only way he could save his child. He didn't want to be selfish like his mother had been his whole life. *Would Tim be able to find his child before it was too late?*

"What are you in deep thought about this morning?" His mother asked.

Tim looked at his mother confused. His mind wasn't all the way there at the moment she asked.

"What?" Tim asked.

"What are you thinking about?" She asked.

He stared at his mother for a few long seconds.

"Are you okay?" She asked.
"Yes, I'm fine." Tim hesitantly replied.

Tim continued to eat.

"So, what were you thinking about?" She asked.
"Nothing. Let it go." He replied.

His mother wasn't happy with that answer. She wasn't satisfied with any answer Tim gave her.

"Why were you dirty?" She asked.
"I fell running." He replied.

She glanced around at his body.

"I don't see marks on you." She said.

He gave his mother a dirty look.

"Where were you all night?" She asked.

Tim gave his mom an angry look.

"How do you know I was gone all night?" He asked.
"Mothers know everything." She replied.

Being mad, Tim wanted to ask her if she knew that he was a killer since she claimed to know everything. He knew that part of him had to remain a secret for the time. Tim needed to concentrate more on where his child could be so he could save it from a horrible destiny.

"I need to go back to work." Tim said.

Tim's mother looked surprised.

"I thought you were going to take more time off?" His mother asked.
"I have taken time off. Now, I have to make money." He replied.

A few minutes later, His mother made a suggestion. She made an offer that she hoped Tim would accept.

"I can help you with money." She said.
"I can make my own money." He said.

Tim only told his mother he had to go back to work. His goal was to get away and find Ava, but his mother didn't need to know the real reason. Money was the least of his worries.

"When do you leave?" His mother asked.
"Tomorrow morning." Tim replied.

They separated after breakfast. Tim had things to do, so his mother left. He decided to stay in the area where he last saw Ava, but he would spend his nights in the wilderness alone and his days walking the city.
The next morning, Tim was woken up by banging on his door. It startled him for a moment.

"Who could it be at this hour?" He thought.

When he answered the door, Tim was handed a search warrant by the police. The officer explained that they had probable cause to search his residence. Tim stood outside nervously while his house was rampaged through. The police never found anything suspicious, which didn't surprise Tim. One of the officers glanced down at his packed bags sitting at the door.

"Are you taking a trip?" The officer asked.
"Yes." Tim replied.
"Where to?" The officer asked.

About that time, his mother showed up. Tim was sure his life would be over at that moment.

"What's going on officer?" His mother asked.
"Stay out of it." Tim said.

The officer intervened.

"Who are you." The officer asked.
"I'm his mother." She replied.

Tim couldn't understand why his mother tried to get involved.

"Can my life get any worse?" Tim thought.

His mother continued to ask the police officer questions. She was worried that her son was in trouble.

"Why are you searching his house?" She asked.
"Ma'am, he's a suspect." The officer replied.

She looked at her son with confusion. She wanted answers, but Tim would give her a hard time.

"What have you done?" She asked.

Tim began to get angry. He wouldn't have this conversation in front of the police officer.

"Are we done here?" He asked the officer.
"Yes, but we will be keeping in touch." The officer replied as he walked away to leave.

His mother wanted to know more.

"What is going on?" She asked Tim.
"Nothing." He replied.

She was upset.

"The police were here searching your house. They don't do that for nothing." She said worried.
"I have to go." Tim said.

Tim threw his bags in the car and left. His mother was upset. She wanted to know what was going on but couldn't get answers out of her son. Staying around Tim's house for a while, she decided to clean up the mess the police had left. At least then her son could come home to a clean place. Still, she would stay determined to find out the truth once her son returned home.

11

Tim went on his journey to search for Ava. With the police on his trail, he wanted to tell Ava everything before he was arrested. She needed to hear the truth from him instead of on television. This would be a chance for her to get the right help for their child since she had decided to keep it. In the meantime, Tim would try to lay low and not kill for a while to avoid the cops being suspicious of him.

After searching for days, Tim became discouraged.

"Where could she be?" He thought.

It had seemed that Tim wouldn't be able to find Ava. This angered him as he continued to search.

"I should have never got involved with anyone." He thought.

Tim began to have thoughts about the choices he had made. He realized he had killed a lot of women in rage. All Tim wanted was a happy life with someone to love. Instead, it always seemed to end in heartache. Every relationship put him back to where he didn't want to be in life.

"It's her fault!" He thought.

He blamed life's misery on his mother. In Tim's mind, it would always be her fault.

"She should have known I would be like this, having a killer dad gives me killer blood." He thought.

The more Tim thought about things, the angrier he became toward his mother for how everything turned out.

"Why didn't she get me help?" Tim thought.

With all the information his mother knew, Tim didn't understand why his mother didn't try to help him. Surely, she knew there was a chance that her son could have carried the killer genes from his biological father. There was no excuse for his mother to ignore that important fact.

After a few more days, Tim began searching again. He focused his mind on trying to save his child from the horrible thoughts he had to hold inside his whole life. The feelings and urges to hurt people became overwhelming at times. Tim was always afraid to let others know because he never wanted to deal with the judgment. He didn't care about what others thought of him anymore. Now, it was about saving his child. Something his mother failed to do.

"If I have to go to prison, Ava will know the truth first so she can get help for our baby." Tim said to himself.

He was determined to do the right thing for the first time in his life. Not even the police could stop him from getting the truth to Ava at this point. If it would cost him his own life, then so be it. As he walked around, Tim observed babies at a park one afternoon in swings.

"What if one of them is my child?" He thought.

The children appeared small to him, but he wasn't sure how old his child was exactly. It had been months since he had thought Ava had given birth.

"Maybe if I wait around her a while, I will see her. Then, I can see my child." Tim thought.

Not wanting to be noticed, he sat across the street on a bench. Tim bought himself a sandwich to eat and something to drink so he wouldn't look suspicious. After a while, a man sat beside him.

"How are you today?" The man asked.
"I'm fine." Tim replied.

A few minutes later,

"It's a nice day." The man said.
"Yes, it is." Tim said.

The man kept glancing over at Tim.

"You don't look familiar. I haven't seen you around. What brings you this way?" The man asked.

Tim had to come up with an excuse. He was getting good at making excuses to cover the truth.

"I travel for work." Tim replied.
"What kind of work?" The man asked.
"I'm a professional photographer. Just traveling around to find work." Tim replied.

The man appeared surprised.

"My brother used to do the same work before he passed." The man said.
"Sorry to hear about his passing." Tim said.

Suddenly, Tim looked over to see Ava walking through the park. He had to go see her.

"I'll see you later." Tim said to the man as he ran off.

"See you around." The man said.

Tim ran across the street toward Ava. He couldn't believe he had finally found her after all this time.

"Ava!" He hollered.

She turned around.

"Tim!" She said excitedly.

They both embraced in a hug.

"I'm so glad I found you." Tim said.
"I'm surprised to see you here." Ava said.

The two stared at each other wondering who was going to start a conversation first. Both had a lot to share.

"I know we didn't leave on good terms last time." Ava said.
"We need to talk." Tim said with his head down.
"Yes, we do. I have something to tell you." Ava said.

Ava wanted to wait for Tim to share his news first. She thought her news would be devastating for him.

"Ava, my father was a killer. He murdered women and went to prison. I worry for our child. I had to come find you." Tim blurted out.

Ava was confused to hear this news from Tim. She was hesitant to respond to anything.

"Tim, I…" Ava said before being interrupted.

"I know how this must sound to you, but you have to get our child help somehow so it doesn't turn out the same way as me and my dad." Tim explained.

She was in shock at the moment.

"Tim! Our baby didn't make it." Ava blurted out.

Now Tim stood in confusion. He had just confessed to being a killer to a woman who he thought had his child. A woman who is now telling him his child is dead. *What would Tim do now?*

"What do you mean?" Tim asked.
"Our baby was dead when it came out. It was a baby girl. She was beautiful." Ava replied.

Tim wasn't sure what to say at the moment. After a few long seconds, he spoke softly.

"What happened?" Tim asked.
"The doctors don't know." Ava replied.

Tim comforted Ava in his arms.

"I'm sorry." Tim said.
"It's not anyone's fault." Ava said.

After a few moments, Ava wondered back to what Tim had blurted out. *Could it be true?*

"What did you mean when you were talking about our child being like you and your dad?" Ava asked.

Tim stared at her in silence. He didn't want to discuss anything further since their child was dead.

"Are you a killer?" Ava asked.
"I was confused. I didn't know what I was saying." Tim replied.

Ava didn't get a good feeling.

"You said your dad was a killer. Are you that serial killer the police are looking for?" Ava asked.
"Ava." Tim said with concern.

She grabbed onto his arm.

"Answer me." Ava said.

Tim stood silently not wanting to engage in the conversation about him being a killer anymore.

"You are. I always felt something off about you. Why didn't you kill me?" Ava asked.

That was a good question for Tim to think about. What was so special about Ava compared to the other women?

"Because I loved you from the first time I saw you sitting on that window." Tim replied.
"We met in the diner. Wait, the night before I had sat outside the window." Ava said.

She began to piece everything together in her mind. Her mind was boggling with thoughts.

"You were stalking me." Ava said in shock.

Ava couldn't believe she had been with a killer that whole time. This took her back to her past. She began to fear a little that he would take her life now that the baby was dead. *But would he?*

"Are you going to kill me now?" She asked.
"I can't. I still love you." Tim replied.

Feeling safe, Ava wasn't sure how to respond to the information she had found out. *Should she go to the police?*

"I'll leave and you never have to see me again." Tim said.

A few seconds later, Ava spoke again.

"Come with me." Ava said.

He never expected her to be okay with what he said.

"Where are we going?" Tim asked.
"I want to show you something." Ava replied.

Tim went with Ava back to her apartment. She pulled out a clipping from an old newspaper article. Tim read it.

"It's about a murderer." Tim said.
"Yes. That was my father. He murdered three women after my mother divorced him. I have been through a lot of therapy." Ava explained.

He thought for a few moments.

"Did you say three women?" Tim asked.
"Yes." Ava replied.

Tim was confused by what Ava was saying. This information wasn't a coincidence to him.

"My mother told me three women too." Tim said.

Ava began to wonder in her mind again. Tim had similar thoughts as they stood together.

"Do you think we may have the same dad?" Ava asked.
"That would mean we are siblings." Tim replied.

It shocked Tim to get this kind of news.

"My dad was with your mom?" Ava asked.
"No, they got the sperm mixed up at the center. My mom was artificially inseminated with me." Tim explained.

Ava thought back to her younger days for a moment. She remembered something her mother once told her.

"My mom said there was a time my dad donated sperm for money. They were going through a hard time. She went back to the place to tell them after he went to prison. They told her they would get rid of his sperm." Ava explained.
"Yeah, they got rid of it inside my mother. I'm living proof." Tim said.

She felt sad for Tim.

"I'm sorry Tim." Ava said.

They both couldn't believe what they discovered. Tim never thought he had a sister out there.

"Now you know the truth about me. I turned out like my father." Tim said.

Ava comforted Tim.

"Maybe it was good that you lost the baby. She would have never had a chance at a good life in this situation." Tim said.
"I don't know what to say." She said.

After a few more moments,

"Just go and never come back. It's only a matter of time before they catch you. I don't want no part of this." Ava said.

Tim looked at Ava.

"I don't want to leave you." He said.

Ava pushed Tim away.

"You have to leave. You are a killer on the run." She said.

Tim left her apartment in a hurry. Since he settled the Ava situation, Tim needed to return home to figure out what to do next. Even though he would never see Ava again, he was happy to know that a sister was out there. Their lives were different. She had help with her issues, unlike Tim who didn't. Ava would always remember Tim, and he would always remember her. Not being so lucky himself, Tim was content with what life had offered on Ava's behalf.

After returning home, Tim felt relieved that he didn't have a child to be concerned about anymore. It was a weight lifted off his shoulders. He needed to focus on how to explain all the killings. The police knew who was doing the killings, they just needed to prove it. Tim had to make sure that no one would find evidence of him. *What would Tim do?*

12

With no worries about a child, Tim thought a small vacation would be good for him. This would give him some time to think more about his next steps and take a break from life again.

"A secluded place is what I need." Tim thought.

His mother came running as soon as she saw Tim arrive home. He dreaded the moment.

"I'm so glad you are home. I was so worried." She claimed.
"I won't be staying home long." Tim stated.

As always, she became curious about her son's next move. She could never let anything rest.

"Where are you going?" She asked.
"Don't worry about it." Tim replied.

Tim walked away to pack. His mother followed him around. This began to annoy Tim. He wanted to be alone.

"Tim! Please talk to me." His mother said.
"About what?" Tim asked.

She decided to take a brave step.

"Are you doing these killings?" His mother hesitantly asked.

Stopping in his tracks, Tim was shocked his mother even asked a question like that. Tim grew angry.

"What would make you think that?" Tim asked.

Being feared by her son, she explained hesitantly. His mother for sure thought it was Tim.

"Well, they said the killer travels, and it seems to happen when you are gone." His mother explained.
"That doesn't prove anything." Tim said.

Tim finished packing his things and set his stuff by the front door. His mother was still bothering him. He tried to ignore her, but the questions kept flowing out of her mouth. Wishing she would mind her own business, Tim continued to walk around trying to get things together.

"What about the police searching your house?" She asked.
"They didn't find any evidence." He said sarcastically.

His mother knew her son was lying. She knew her son was guilty of something and it worried her.

"What are you hiding?" She asked.
"Stay out of my life!" Tim yelled.

Tim was tired of being questioned and watched every day by his mother. They would have had a good relationship if she chose to be truthful. Tim felt like it wasn't his fault that everything turned out the way it did. He had more important things to address at the moment than to argue with his mother.

"I'm not leaving until you tell me the truth." His mother said.

Tim turned to look at her angrily. He thought she was going a little too far with things.

"Don't push me over the edge." Tim stated.
"You wouldn't hurt me." She said firmly.

With confident,

"How do you know?" Tim asked.
"I'm your mother!" She said loudly.

At that moment, something changed in Tim. He couldn't hold back the anger he felt toward his mother.

"I am the killer everyone is talking about! I killed all of the women one by one! Your son is a killer! How does that make you feel?" Tim asked.

His mother stood in shock. She never thought it could be true. *Did Tim just confess to his mother?*

"I can get you some help." She claimed.
"You should have done that a long time ago instead of keeping your little secret!" Tim yelled.

She was extremely upset at this point. Her son had taken the secret thing too far at this point.

"This is not my fault. Let me help you." She said.
"It's too late!" Tim said in anger.

He grabbed a hold of his mother and began to choke her. She struggled to breathe while his hands gripped tighter. She couldn't believe her son was going to try to kill his mother.

"Tim, please." She begged gasping for air.

Not listening, Tim watched while his mother died by his hands. She was murdered by her son.

"I told you not to push me." Tim whispered.

When he came to his senses, Tim realized he had killed her. *What would he do now?* He had to come up with a plan quickly before anyone saw what had happened. Waiting until after nightfall, Tim dragged his mother through the woods to his victim's graveyard. There, he chose to bury her. Not with his victims, but near them in the woods. He didn't think she deserved a spot with the victims.

After digging a deep hole, Tim rolled his mother's body into it and covered her with dirt. Then, he sat with his victims for a while. He started feeling sorrow as he thought back on his life once more.

"Why didn't she just mind her own business?" He thought.

Tim didn't want to kill his mother, but she pushed him over his boundaries. With all the anger inside, he couldn't control anything that happened. She had found out he was a killer, so Tim had to silence her somehow anyway. His mother would expose him at that point.

"She ruined my life." Tim whispered.

Not knowing how to fix anything in his life, Tim felt alone. Eventually, he realized there wasn't anything he could do. With his mother gone now, Tim could focus on his next steps in life. Returning to the house, he showered and went to bed. Waking early the next morning, Tim sat for breakfast by himself. He was used to his mother being there asking questions.

"I have to get out of here." He thought.

He grabbed his bags and left. Looking back through his mirrors, he could imagine his mother seeing him go. *Would this killing haunt him?* Tim had hoped not, but wasn't sure anymore.

"*It's her fault she is dead.*" Tim thought.

Should his mother have kept a secret like that from him? Tim continued with thoughts while driving to his destination. Once there, he settled in and relaxed for a while by himself.

"*Finally, peace and quiet.*" He thought.

For the next few days, Tim reflected on life. Things happened that he felt were out of his control. He couldn't change the past. There was nothing to do but move forward. *How would he do this?*

"*Maybe I can move, but where?*" He thought.

After some research, Tim found an old cabin for sale secluded in the woods in another state.

"*This could be my chance to start over.*" He thought.

He left for a couple of days to look at the old cabin. It needed work, but Tim thought it was perfect. Being confident, Tim knew he could do the work himself. After making an offer, he returned to his vacation cabin. Planning more, Tim decided he would secretly move his victim's graveyard with him if the offer went through. As for work, he had enough savings to live on for a while. He would find another traveling photography company to work for if he had to. It was set. Tim would move if the deal was made. There was no turning back now.

While still on his mini vacation, Tim enjoyed the lake. Fishing and relaxing were two things he mostly did to pass his days. One evening, he sat out to observe the sunset. As the stars began to appear, He heard voices.

"Who is out there?" Tim thought.

As he followed the voices, Tim stumbled upon a campsite. A group of people were out staying in the woods. Tim kept his distance out of site. He didn't want anyone to see him.

"I better get back to my cabin." Tim thought.

Tim returned to go to bed. He slept well into the next morning. It was the last day of his trip, so he decided to go hiking. During his walk, he stumbled across a creek with a waterfall. It was beautiful. Tim stood admiring the fall for quite a while, when suddenly, he saw a woman come out of the woods and climb into the creek. It looked as if she were searching for something. Being curious, Tim walked around to give his assistance to the woman.

"Can I help you with something?" Tim asked.
"Yes. I'm looking for my bracelet. I swam here earlier with my friends. It must have fell off in the water." She replied.

Tim decided to offer some assistance.

"Do you want me to help you look?" Tim asked.
"That would be nice. Look around on the ground while I search the waters." The woman replied.

The woman continued to search under the waters. Tim began looking around on the ground.

"It has to be here somewhere." The woman said as she continued to walk the waters and look.

A few moments later, Tim saw something by the edge of the water. He picked up a bracelet.

"Is this it?" Tim asked.

The woman raised her head toward Tim. She couldn't believe he had actually found her bracelet.

"Yes! That's it!" She said excitedly as she began to run out of the waters not paying attention.

All of a sudden, the woman tripped and fell onto a rock hitting her head. Tim stood in silence observing. She wasn't moving. Nervousness grew over him quickly as he tried to figure out what to do.

"Are you okay" Tim asked.

No response out of the woman.

"Miss?" He blurted out softly.

Tim stepped slowly over to her. He could see blood draining from her head into the water.

"What should I do?" He asked himself.

He grew concerned that someone would see him there with her. This was an accident, but the police may have thought differently.

"I have to leave." Tim thought.

Leaving the woman unconscious in the water, he panicked and ran back to his cabin. Tim didn't want anyone to think he hurt her. With everything that was happening around him, he had to remain careful. Later, Tim noticed he had the woman's bracelet on him. This concerned him. He would have to return it somehow. As he was leaving the next day, a neighbor approached him.

"A woman was found dead early this morning at the falls." The man said.
"Really?" Tim asked.

He pretended to be concerned.

"Yes. It appears she busted her head on a rock. She must have fallen." The man explained.

Tim continued loading his car to leave. He didn't want to raise suspicion with the neighbor.

"Sorry to hear that. I have to be going now. I have an appointment with a client." Tim said as he drove away in his car.

He didn't want to stick around the scene for police to show up. Once he returned home, Tim pulled out the bracelet.

"I can't keep this. I'll bury it next to my mother. It will stay hidden there." Tim thought.

That's what he did. Waiting until almost dark, Tim walked through the woods to his mother's grave. Making sure no one followed, he dug a hole next to his mother's body and buried the bracelet.

"I didn't kill this one mom. This was a complete accident. I know you probably wouldn't believe me, but it's the truth." Tim whispered to his mother as if she were listening.

A while later, Tim walked back to his house. He ate and went to bed. Shortly after falling asleep, Tim began having a nightmare. In this dream, his mother was shaming him for not trying to help the woman.

"I couldn't help her!" He screamed as he woke up.
Glancing around the room, he was confused.

"What is going on?" He asked himself.

Tim was shaking and sweating. Quickly, he glanced more around the room to realize it had just been a dream. Not being able to sleep well, Tim thought about the woman most of the night.

"Why didn't I help her?" He thought.

Fear is what kept him from saving the woman. Fear of being caught, fear of being blamed. Tim knew the police suspected him, so he wanted to stay out of the spotlight when it came to tragedies.

"It was for the best." He thought.

Tim thought that his mother should understand why he did the things he had done in his life. *Why did he care so much what his mother thought now?* Moving forward, he would try to live more quietly. He knew he shouldn't have offered the woman help to begin with. She would have eventually found her bracelet without him. *Would Tim have killed her anyway?*

Over the next week, Tim would remain indoors and out of trouble until he decided it was time to continue with life. He had to give his killings a rest, or risk being caught. The jail wasn't where he wanted to be.

13

Tim thought back to when he was with Ava. Even though they were related, he still couldn't get the times they were intimate and closed off his mind. He needed that kind of intimacy more with someone. Killings weren't enough for him now. He had an urge for more sexual activity but had to be careful not to leave evidence. *Would Tim now be a rapist-killer?*

Becoming bored with time, Tim thought it would be a good idea to return to work. He set everything up for his next job and journeyed off the next day. While at his job area, he met a woman who was at the event. Even though Tim didn't like associating with one's who attended the events he worked at, he found this one quite interesting. Deciding to interact, he wanted to see where this relationship led them. Maybe it would be good for him in the long run.

"Hello." She said.
"Hi." Tim responded.

Tim continued with his job.

"Do you attend a lot of events?" She asked.
"Quite a few." He replied.

Glancing around the room, she thought the event could use a little excitement. Everyone appeared to be content talking with each other. She was more on the wild side of life.

"This is not one of my favorite events to attend." She said.
"Why not?" Tim asked.

The woman rolled her eyes.

"Don't you think it's a little boring?" She asked.
"I'm just here to do my job." Tim replied.

She saw something interesting in Tim and wanted to get to know more about him. *Would Tim like this?*

"What's your name?" She asked.

He was hesitant at first.

"Tim." He replied.
"I'm Kara." She said.
"Nice to meet you." He said.

At first, she was very talkative and friendly. They met up on several occasions after the party event. Tim felt complete around her. He thought maybe this would be his chance to get intimate with someone.

"Could she be the one for me?" Tim thought.

After a while, she became interested in Tim's life. He was a private person, so he controlled how much information he told her. If he told her too much, she would figure his life out.

"Tell me about your life." She said.

He was hesitant to tell her anything.

"Nothing to tell. I am a traveling photographer." Tim said.

She knew there was more to him than he was telling.

"Tell me more." She said.
"Like what?" Tim asked.

Tim didn't like discussing himself much. He felt that Kara was wanting to know too much.

"Have you ever been married?" She asked.
"Once." Tim replied.

She was curious why they were not together anymore.

"Why did you divorce?" She asked.

He stared at her for a few seconds debating on whether to tell her his story. *Would Tim tell her everything?*

"Who said I divorced?" Tim asked.

This surprised her at the moment.

"So, you are still married?" She asked.

After a few long seconds, Tim replied.

"My wife died giving birth to our child." He replied.
"Sorry, I didn't know." She said.

She felt bad that he had lost his wife. She tried to turn the conversation away from the deaths.

"Is your child back home with your mother?" She asked.

Tim glanced at her wondering why she was so interested in his life.

"My child died at birth with my wife. I lost them both that day." Tim explained.

In shock,

"That's awful." She said.
"That's life. Some people get to live, while others die." He said.

The woman didn't know what to think when she heard Tim say it that way. He appeared content about death. This freaked her out a little, but she stayed calm with conversation.

"What about your parents?" Kara asked.
"Both are dead." Tim replied.

Kara was silent. Tim thought she was asking too many questions. He didn't like sharing information about his life.

"So, you lost your wife, child, father, and mother?" She asked.

Tim shrugged his shoulders.

"I told you there was nothing to tell." Tim replied.

The friendship between the two appeared to be awkward. Tim didn't think it would work. Kara was asking a lot of questions when they met up and it reminded him of his mother over time.

"I don't like her anymore." Tim thought.

Now, he needed to figure out if he wanted to continue meeting with her. When he traveled, she would come. They were friends, but she wanted to be in his life too much. His mother was the same way when she was alive. The only place she never went to was his house. He kept women away from his home. This ensured no one would find out about him.

"How come you never take me to your house?" Kara asked.
"I don't like anyone there." Tim replied.

Kara thought Tim was hiding something that he didn't want her to know. She would continue to ask questions to find out the real reason he didn't want her at his house. Tim would be bothered by this.

"Do you have a girlfriend there?" She asked.
"No!" Tim replied angrily.

Kara looked at Tim. She was surprised to see him get angry so easily. This was a side she hadn't seen of him before.

"Look, I'm a private person. Stop questioning me." Tim said.
"Sorry." Kara said.

A few minutes later,

"Maybe we shouldn't see each other for a while." Tim suggested.
"Why not?" She asked.

Tim said something without thinking first.

"I wouldn't want you to end up like my mother." Tim replied.

Kara became nervous.

"What do you mean?" She asked.

Silently gazing into her eyes, Tim could see himself killing Kara. Holding control, he knew it would be risky because people had seen them together all the time. So, Tim had to make himself leave.

"I have to go." He said.

She tried to stop him.

"Wait!" She hollered.
"No! Leave me alone." He said as he walked off.

Tim returned home that evening. He was happy with his choice to walk away from Kara. She was his mother made over. There would have been no way he could deal with the questioning all the time. It had been a while since Tim visited his victim's graveyard, so he decided to take the walk through the woods while it was dark. It appeared more creepier than before as he slowly approached the area. The night air was thick and the trees had lost most of their leaves. Suddenly, the noise of twigs breaking in the woods beside him caught his attention.

"Who's there?" He hollered out.

There was no answer. Tim shrugged it off as if it were an animal. After a few moments, he heard it again. This time, it was closer and louder. The sounds startled him and he turned to look.

"Who's there?" He repeated.

Looking into the darkness, he could see a woman figure. This raised his brows. Tim wasn't sure what it was at first.

"It's one of my victims haunting me." He thought.

Suddenly, the shadowy figure began walking toward him. Tim became nervous as he watched it approaching closer.

"Who could it be?" Tim wondered.

Then, a voice spoke out.

"What is this place?" The voice asked.

Tim recognized the voice of the shadowy figure.

"Kara?" Tim asked.
"Who else would it be?" Kara asked as she stepped in front of Tim.

Confused as to why she was there, Tim asked questions back.

"Did you follow me home?" He asked.
"Yes." She replied.

He stared at her.

"Why?" He asked.
"I wanted to see where you were from and why you stayed secretive about your life." She replied.

This didn't go over well with Tim. After a moment, Kara began asking questions. She was curious about Tim.

"So, what is this place?" She asked.
"This is my private area to hang out in the woods and think." Tim replied.

Curiously, she checked everything out.

"Why are all these stones in a circle?" She asked.
"Let's go back to the house." Tim said.

He stood to walk back to the house with Kara, but she wanted to know more about his area.

"Wait, these look like grave markings." She said as she leaned over to observe the stones.

Kara was on dangerous turf. Tim was already discouraged that she followed him home. Now, she was uncovering his life. This made him angry inside. He wanted her to leave.

"Get away from here!" Tim angrily blurted out.

Kara Leaned up in fear. She knew he was angry at her.

"What is buried here?" She asked.
"This is my victim graveyard." Tim replied.

In shock,

"What?" Kara asked.
"See, I'm a killer. I have killed many women like you." Tim explained.

Kara appeared confused as she thought for a moment. Then, she figured it out in her mind.

"You're the killer that has been traveling around killing all them women." She said.
"Bingo!" Tim hollered out sarcastically.

In fear, Kara knew she had to get out of there.

"I will leave." Kara pleaded.
"There's one problem with that. You know my secret now." Tim said.

She had to think fast.

"I won't tell anyone." She pleaded more.

Tim grabbed her around the throat.

"You are going to join the others." He said softly while watching the fear in Kara's eyes.

Kara continued to plea for her life as she gasped for a breath each time she spoke. It was too late for her. She made the mistake of following him home and then through the woods. Now, she discovered the truth about him and put her own life in jeopardy.

Tim couldn't control himself once the kill began. He looked at her as if she were another one of his victims. Nothing could stop him in the moment. She should have left Tim alone like he wanted instead of prying into his business. His mother learned the hard way, and now Kara would.

"She has to pay the consequences for her actions." Tim thought.

Once she was dead, Tim buried her next to his mother.

"Here you go, mom. I found your twin. She's just like you." Tim whispered.

He went back to the house to shower and go to bed. The next morning, Tim walked outside to see a car in his driveway. After a moment, he realized it was Kara's car. Now, he had to get rid of it fast. Tim drove it miles away from his home to abandon it in the woods. Then, he walked home. It took him until nightfall to return home. Being exhausted, he decided to eat and go to bed for the night.

14

The phone rang and awoke Tim out of bed in the early hours. This didn't go over well with him.

"Who could this be?" He thought.

It was the Realtor telling him that he was approved for the isolated cabin in the woods he applied for. After the payment was made, Tim could move in. He grew excited at the idea.

"I forgot all about it." Tim thought.

He would meet with the Realtor right away and get the funds transferred. When everything was signed and complete, he began making arrangements for the move. This was a fresh start in his mind. He would work a few more big jobs before retiring completely. He wasn't old enough to retire but had the funds to. Wanting to use his time to focus on an isolated life away from society. Also, he could avoid the police since they knew where he had lived before.

"The police wouldn't be able to find me out there hidden in the woods at my new place." He thought.

With the keys in his hands, Tim started packing everything. He couldn't wait to move and begin his new life. After days of packing, he decided to load his car with what he could and take it over to the new cabin. He arrived at the cabin right before nightfall, where he unloaded his things. It was late, so he settled in for the night after carrying his things in.

"I'll spend the night here." He thought.

The first night went well. Tim went to the store to get paint the next day. Then, he spent a few days painting the whole cabin. This helped keep his mind off killing. Cleaning the cabin completely from top to bottom took another week. Eventually, Tim moved a few more loads to his new home. Then, moved the big things with a trailer he had sitting around.

"Almost complete." He thought.

He was satisfied with the way the inside of the cabin was looking. Now, he wanted to focus on the outside. He spent the next few weeks painted the exterior, cleaning up the yard areas, and moving fallen branches from trees near the home. He made a big fire pit to burn wood. Tim was almost satisfied. There was one more thing he needed to decide. Something very important to him that he would never leave behind. He would begin planning.

"Where will I put my victim graveyard?" He thought.

Tim walked into the woods to find the perfect place to bury his victim pictures. He didn't want it too close to the house in case others showed up. It had to be out of sight to visitors. Tim wanted to be the only one to know about it. After a while of observing through the woods, he found the perfect spot. The area had big trees that were similar to the ones at the old place.

"This looks like a great spot for a graveyard." He thought.

Now that everything else was finished, he had to carefully move his graveyard to the new spot without being caught. Then, things would be complete for him. He returned to his old home to begin the process. While there, he received a phone call. Tim's job was short of help and needed him to work. Not what he wanted to do at the time. Tim agreed, so he decided to hold off on the rest of the move and ventured out to his job site.

"I will move the graveyard when I return." He thought.

Everything went well with the job. Tim completed the event within a few days and was ready to leave the next day. He went out to get food late into the evening. On the way back to his hotel, he passed a woman who caught his attention. Instantly, he turned to follow while eating his food. Following her for a while, she eventually walked through an alley.

"It's time." Tim thought.

Still wearing his camera, Tim decided to use the strap on the camera to strangle her. She looked strong to him, so he didn't want to take any chances of her fighting and getting away. After she went out, he admired her. He noticed she wasn't breathing. Realizing he choked her too tight, Tim was angry she was dead so soon. Deciding to leave, he took a quick picture before he left. There was no reason to pose her naked when she was already gone.

"I didn't get what I wanted this time." Tim said to himself.

Tim wanted another naked pose for his collection but didn't get it. Things happened differently because he lost too much control of himself this time. This would not be one of his normal killings. He didn't like the change that happened on occasion. Tim only had one way of killing that he enjoyed.

"Next time." He thought.

Leaving out the next day, he wasn't satisfied. Tim would find another victim on the way back home. Stopping at a gas station right before his exit, he saw a woman walking around talking to people. This could be his opportunity. Approaching him, he wondered what she wanted.

"Can you give me a ride?" She asked.

Tim wasn't sure about this.

"A ride where?" He asked.
"Up a few exits." She replied.

He didn't want to.

"I just came from there." He said.
"I'll pay you." She said.

Tim thought while he continued to pump gas. He saw it as a sign that this was the one.

"Get in." He said.
"Thank you!" She said excitedly.

He glanced around to make sure no one was looking before he drove off with the woman.

"I appreciate the ride." She said.
"You're welcome." Tim said.

After a few moments, the woman leaned over to Tim's lap and began unbuttoning his pants.

"What are you doing?" He asked.

She smiled at him.

"I told you I would pay you." She replied.

Before Tim could say anything else, the woman was performing oral sex on him. He began to lose concentration on his driving, so he pulled off onto a dark road. He enjoyed every minute of the woman's performance. Afterward, he sat catching his breath. This was satisfying.

"How was it?" She asked.

Tim couldn't speak.

"It was that good?" She asked.
"Yes." Tim replied.

A few moments later,

"Have you ever had a woman do that to you?" She asked.
"No." He replied.

The woman chuckled.

"What's funny?" Tim asked.

She glanced at him.

"You are the first grown man that's never had oral sex performed on him." She replied.
"I don't find anything funny about that." Tim said.

She shrugged her shoulders at Tim.

"Have you had sex with a woman?" She asked.
"Yes." He replied.
"Must have lame without oral. Maybe I can give your wife lessons." She said.

Tim stared at her as she continued with laughter. He opened his door to get out of the car.

"Where are you going?" She asked.

He didn't answer her. Tim walked into the darkness. After a while, the woman exited the car.

"Where are you?" She asked.

Nothing was heard except the sounds of the crickets chirping in the night air. The darkness blinded her surroundings.

"Hey!" She hollered.
"Where are you?" She asked.

There was no reply.

"This isn't funny." She said.

The woman didn't know what to do. It was dark and scary to her. She began walking down the road by herself.

"I can't believe he ditched me like this. What a jerk. He could have at least dropped me at my exit." She thought.

What the woman didn't know, Tim was following behind her in the darkness. He didn't like the fact that she laughed at him. She was about a half mile away from the car when Tim went in for the kill. He strangled her with his hands, putting her to sleep. Her body on the ground, Tim dragged her closer to the woods. There, he stripped her clothes off and posed her body.

"I will finally get a satisfying picture." He thought.

She began to awake after Tim took the picture he wanted. The girl was confused as to why Tim had taken a picture.

"What are you doing?" She asked.

Tim knelt beside her slowly. He wanted to put fear in her for laughing at him like she did.

"I'm going to kill you." Tim said as he put his hands around her throat.

She tried to holler out, but no one could hear her. Her screams echoed through the darkness. After strangling her, Tim walked back to his car to leave. A man stopped his car beside Tim's car.

"Everything okay?" He asked.
"Yes." Tim replied.

A few seconds later,

"I didn't know if you were having car trouble." The man said.
"Potty break, couldn't hold it." Tim said.

The man was convinced.

"Well, have a good night." the man said as he drove off.

That was close. If the guy had shown up a minute earlier, Tim would have been caught. He drove to the old house where he spent a few days. Planning the process to relocate the gravesite. Taking a shower, Tim relaxed for the rest of the night. The next day, his phone rang. It was his aunt.

"Have you seen your mother?" She asked.

Tim decided to lie to her.

"Yes. We had breakfast together this morning and then she went shopping." He replied.

This would surely throw her off for a while. She wasn't so convinced that Tim was being honest.

"I haven't heard from her in a while. That's not like her." She said.
"We have been spending a lot of time together lately. She's just been busy." He said.

She thought for a moment.

"I'm glad to hear this. I know she wanted to have a better relationship with you." She said.
"Yes, things have been going well." Tim said.

They said their good-byes and hung the phone up. Tim bought himself some time to get his graveyard moved before his aunt came searching for his mother again. He needed to work fast.

"When she comes, I'll be gone already." He thought.

Tim made his way to his victim graveyard with a box. He dug each grave and put everything he had buried into the box. Tim even included the stones for the grave markings. He had a unique one for each grave. As he walked away, Tim glanced over to where his mother was buried.

"I'm moving and I'm not taking you with me. Good-bye mom." He said.

He decided to leave his mother behind along with the memories of the past. After loading the box into his car, Tim drove to the new location. He wanted to wait until daylight so he could see to make everything perfect. Tim carried the box into his little cabin for the night and went to sleep.

Later, he had a nightmare again. In this dream, someone had stolen his box. Tim woke up frantically searching. A few moments went by before he came to and realized that it was just a dream. With daylight approaching, he decided to stay up for the rest of the night. His goal was to work at his new graveyard site for the day. It needed to be complete before anyone had come by the cabin.

When it was time, he carried the box to the new site. He was ready to create his new victim graveyard. Tim dug his holes and buried his stuff from the victims. He cleaned up around the area and placed everything the way he wanted. To him, he accomplished a lot since buying the cabin.

"This looks great." He thought.
"Now, it's complete." He whispered.

Tim felt proud and content with his new life. The fact that he was secluded from society, made him happy. He was alone, no one to bother him, was surrounded by nature, had his graveyard. *What more could he want?*

"This is an awesome life." He thought.

Tim spent money stalking up on foods for his cabin. He used the falling trees to build a small storage shed to store the foods in. It was enough to last him for a while. Also, he learned how to grow a garden. This would be the new life for him. He enjoyed the new life for a while and learned more survival skills in the process. There wasn't anything he couldn't do to survive alone. He didn't want for nothing. As long as he could keep his urges under control, Tim would live forever where he was at.

15

As time went on, Tim grew eager to explore the woods further. Even though not all of it was his, he still decided to hike the narrow trails. Some of it led to public walking paths through nature. Each day, Tim observed different areas. He wanted an idea of what was around him. One late afternoon, he sat on a small hillside watching people walk one of the paths. His killing urges grew seeing multiple women pass with their partners. They appeared too loving in Tim's eyes.

"Look how happy in love they are." He thought.
"I wish I could be as happy as them." He said to himself.

Tim was getting ready to start hiking back to his cabin when he noticed a woman walking alone slowly. She stopped every few seconds looking out beyond the trees. It was as if she were in deep thought about something.

"I wonder what's on her mind." Tim thought.

Moving in closer, he became curious about her. Tim stepped out onto the path. The woman was only steps away.

"Are you okay?" Tim asked.
"Yes, just observing nature." She replied.
"I love nature also." Tim said.

The woman nodded and smiled.

"I work at a nature preserve center." She said.

Tim thought that was interesting.

"I'm a photographer." Tim said.
"Do you have any pictures of nature?" She asked.
"No. I do events that I travel to." He replied.

The two grew much interest in each other.

"Do you live around here?" She asked.
"Yes, back through those woods." Tim replied pointing behind him.

The woman glanced back.

"You should come check out the nature center in town sometime." She said.
"I will." Tim said.

A few moments went by before they went their separate ways.

"Well, I have to get back to town. I'll see you later." She said.

A few weeks went by without seeing the woman. Tim sat on the hillside, but she never appeared. Assuming he would never see her again, he spent his time on gathering wood for the coming winter months. He kept it piled beside the cabin. Later, he built a shelter for the wood pieces to be stacked under to help keep it dry from the rain.

"I will be warm this winter." He thought.

Early one evening, Tim decided to clean the chimney out. He climbed onto the roof to check everything out.

"It all looks good to me." He said to himself.

As he began climbing down the ladder, Tim noticed something off with a piece of wood on the side of the cabin.

"What's this?" He thought.

Tim removed the wood carefully. Inside a little hole, was a piece of paper. He opened it slowly. The paper had directions wrote on it, kind of like a map. This became interesting to him.

"I wonder where these leads?" He thought.

After putting the ladder up, Tim took the piece of paper inside. It was too late to be exploring that night, so he waited until the next day. He lied curiously of what he had discovered.

"I will follow this tomorrow and see what I find." Tim thought.

He could barely sleep through the night. Being anxious, Tim wanted to know what was out there. He knew nothing about the previous owner.

"What could he have hidden?" Tim whispered to himself.

After breakfast, Tim left to adventure through the woods. He followed the map's direction. Miles later, Tim came to the end of the directions. He glanced around, looking for any evidence of something hidden or buried.

"There has to be something here." He thought.

There wasn't anything obvious in sight, so Tim began walking the area. On the other side of a mount, he found an opening.

"What's this?" He whispered to himself.

It looked like a big hole to crawl through. Tim wondered what could be inside, but it was dark. He didn't have any lights, so he decided to come back another day with flashlights. That would help him see where the hole led. As he began to walk away, he noticed a shirt laying on the ground.

"Who's is this?" He thought as he picked it up.

Not being sure where the shirt had come from, Tim threw it to the side and walked on. He ventured back home exploring along the way. As he approached his cabin, Tim saw the woman he met on the path weeks prior. She was snooping around the area. He became curious as to why she was there.

"What are you doing here?" Tim asked.

The woman turned around quickly. Tim startled her.

"I remembered you saying you lived this way. I came to see if I could find you." She replied.
"I'm a little busy at the moment." Tim said.

Tim stepped up onto his front porch approaching his front door. He really didn't want company.

"I wanted to invite you to town tomorrow. We are having an exhibit event at the nature center." She explained.

He turned around to politely decline.

"I have things to do around here, but thank you for the invite." Tim said.
"Okay, well, maybe some other time. I'll see you later." She said as she walked off into the woods.

The following day, Tim wasn't feeling well. He stayed around the cabin sleeping. This lasted a few days. A week later, he decided to go check on his graveyard. Getting close, he could see the back of a woman kneeling next to one of the grave markings. He became curious.

"Who are you?" He asked loudly.

When the woman turned around, he could see that it was the nature woman that had stopped by.

"Why are you here?" He asked.
"I wanted to check out these unique stones I stumbled upon after leaving last week." She replied.

Tim began to get angry.

"No one is supposed to be here!" He said.

The woman took a few steps back.

"These stones are unique." She said.
"This is my private property." Tim said.

She wondered why Tim was acting suspicious.

"What's buried here?" She asked curiously.
"I told you, no one is supposed to be here." Tim said.

He lounged out at the woman grabbing her roughly around the neck. She tried to fight him off, but was unsuccessful. Tim strangled her, putting her to sleep. Then, he got an idea.

"I'll pose her for a picture in the graveyard. That will be beautiful." He whispered to himself.

Running back to the cabin for his camera, Tim knew he had to hurry before she awoke. After finding it, he took his camera back to the graveyard just in time before she awoke.

"What are you doing?" The woman asked as she began waking up.

Once more, Tim choked her out again. Then, ripped her clothes off and posed her for a picture.

"This picture is a telling story." He thought.

Perfectly, he posed her body next to his grave markings. After taking the picture, he admired her body. Beginning to get aroused, he decided to rape her. During the rape, she woke up and tried to fight him. He pinned her to the ground where he held her. There was nothing she could do.

"Stop!" she yelled.

No one could hear her. It was only the two of them in the woods for miles. When the rape was finished, Tim strangled her until she took her last breath. Now, he had to figure out how to clean up his mess. *Would he bury her?* Thinking on it, Tim had a different idea than burying her. She had his semen evidence inside her, so he dragged her body back to his cabin along with her things.

"I'll burn her." He thought.

After throwing wood into his big fire pit, Tim started a fire. Rolling her body into it, he tossed her things on top of her. Everything was burned. Later into the evening with the fire burning out, there was nothing left except bones. They would be the new addition to his victim graveyard along with her picture once he developed it.

"I will bury her bones so no one sees them." He thought.

A few days passed before Tim decided to follow the map back out to the hole he found. Once he arrived, Tim began crawling his way through the hole opening. With flashlights on, he could see a short distance ahead of him. The hole eventually became bigger the farther he crawled. When Tim could stand, he observed around. It was a hidden cave underground.

"This is amazing." Tim thought.

The inside of the cave was beautiful. This would become a good hide out place if he ever needed one. It even had a nice area he could bury his treasures. The cave was definitely a cool place to explore. Over the next few weeks, Tim began setting up the inside of the cave with lights and everything, in case he would have to resort to staying there. He loved the cave so much, that he would spend occasional nights in it. Having this second place to go made Tim happy.

"Life couldn't be better." He thought.

Eventually, Tim made the decision to go back to work. He had a lot accomplished with his life. Tim was ready to make more money. Also, he needed to think about getting his old house sold. The money could be used to increase his food storage. Tim could even start storing foods out in the cave too.

His cravings became strong again to kill. After completing a photo job, he went for a stroll through town. He passed a bar a few times. It didn't seem too busy, so Tim went inside for a quick drink. After sitting for a while, the bartender began a conversation with him.

"Passing through?" She asked.
"Something like that." Tim replied.
"Where you from?" She asked.

Tim didn't answer. The bartender woman was suspicious of him. With the news that had went around about a serial killer, she became cautious and protective of the bar and costumers.

"Look, we don't like trouble around here." She said.

Tim glanced up at her.

"Am I causing trouble?" He asked.

The woman thought for a moment.

"You're not from around here. We always keep an eye on the newbies. There's a killer out there somewhere." She replied.

Not liking what he just heard, Tim politely stood up. He knew it was time to leave or there would be trouble.

"Have a great evening." He said to the bartender.

She watched him leave the bar. Later that night, she cleaned everything up and closed. On the way out, she carried the trash out. Tim stepped out from behind the dumpster.

"I thought you left." She said.

Tim stood in silence as he stared into her eyes. She began to fear what Tim would do to her.

"You need to leave or I'll call the cops." She said.

He reached out to grab her around the neck, but she swung her arm to block it. They began wrestling as Tim tried to gain control over her. She was a fighter and eventually got away from him. Tim ran into the darkness as she went to call the police. Leaving the area that night, he would return home where no one would find him. The woman went to the station and gave a description of her attacker. It resembled him. They put the picture on television with every news station. *What would he do now?*

"I'll have to hide out here for a while." Tim thought.

It was the middle of the night before Tim arrived home. Being tired, he washed up and went to bed. Tim spent the next day thinking about how careless he had been lately. For a short time, he thought that maybe he should stop killing. It was only a matter of time before it caught up with him anyway. Eventually, Tim decided he didn't care. He would kill until he was stopped.

"What do I have to lose?" He thought.

He continued, killing five more women over the next few months. Each of them added to his victim graveyard. One night after killing a woman, he heard a noise behind him. As he turned around, he saw a homeless man standing behind him. This would be a witness.

"Great, now I have to kill him." He thought.

Tim quickly ran after the man. He had to kill him since the man saw what happened. This would be the first male victim to die by Tim's hands. All of his victim's so far have been females.

"I won't tell anyone." The man pleaded.

It was too late for him. Tim had already gone in for the kill. He strangled the man until he died. Then, he left both the woman and man lying lifeless on the ground and left the scene. Back home early the next morning, Tim decided to take a break from work. This would give him time to spend by himself again until his urges to kill grew once more. *Would it ever end?*

16

Tim didn't know the police officers had put a tracking device on his car back when they searched his old home. It was part of the search warrant that Tim refused to read. The police had been tracking everywhere he drove, but they couldn't track where he walked. This gave them an idea of what areas he was in at the time of the murders, but still didn't prove that he was the actual killer.

After doing some investigation, they knew Tim was in the same areas at the time of each recent killing. Also, the detectives pulled his cell phone records and knew he was in the prior areas that the past women were murdered. They were certain Tim was the killer. It would take the police a while of working hard to build a case against Tim before they could go in for an arrest.

One thing the police officers didn't know, there were more women than they originally thought. Tim buried the women that were just missing. They would have to connect him to these murders somehow if the bodies were ever found. *Could the police convince Tim to confess to everything once they arrested him?* Things were getting out of hand when he committed murders. With Tim getting careless with his killings, he would be caught soon.

Tim traveled back to his old house to clean it. He thought it was time he sold the house and be done completely with the past. While there one day, his aunt came to visit him.

"Where have you been?" She asked.
"Working." He replied.

She thought for a second. Tim was away from home quite a bit at times and his aunt knew her sister became upset about it.

"You work quite a lot." She said.
"Yes." He said.

She glanced around the room and noticed everything was gone. This made her curious.

"Why is your house empty?" She asked.
"I moved." He replied.

Being curious, she continued. She wanted to know more about where Tim had escaped to.

"Where?" She asked.
"That's no concern to you." He replied.

His aunt knew Tim was the rude type at times, so she didn't argue with him. All she wanted was to find her sister.

"Well, I have been here several times and I can't find your mother." She explained.
"I'm sure you will see her soon." Tim replied.

Tim showed no concern. His aunt was worried that Tim didn't care about his mother's life.

"Have you seen her lately." She asked.
"No." He replied.

Being discouraged, his aunt knew Tim was hiding something from her. She wanted answers.

"Where is she at?" She asked.
"Who?" He asked.

She was becoming upset at his nonsense. His aunt knew Tim was hiding something from her.

"Your mother." She replied.
"She could be in the woods." He replied.
"Your mother doesn't go walking through the woods alone." She said.

He looked at his aunt with an evil glare in his eyes. Tim never liked to be questioned so much.

"She's not a child." He said.
"I just want to know where my sister is. I am worried that something has happened to her." She said.

Tim was growing angrier by the minute. He didn't understand why his aunt was bothering him.

"Instead of questioning me, go look for her. I am not my mother's keeper." He suggested.
"I have looked for her and she is nowhere to be found. That should concern you." She said.

Not caring at the moment, Tim had things to get done. He didn't have time for any interruptions.

"I'm busy. I have to get everything cleaned up to sell this house. You need to leave." Tim said.
"I'm sure you are." She sarcastically said.

After a few moments, his aunt made a threat that Tim didn't like hearing. This pushed him over the edge.

"I'm going to the police and make a missing person report. They will question you." She said.
"Now, you have crossed the line." He said.

He became angry. He thought his aunt should mind her own business. Then again, she was related to his mother so Tim knew it was in their blood to intrude on other's lives. Tim grabbed his aunt from behind and tied her up. Also, he taped her mouth shut. Then, he leaned over her.

"I don't know why you couldn't have minded your own business. Now you have to die just like my mother." Tim said.

As he went to strangle her, there was a knock at the door. He left his aunt to see who it was.

"Who could it be now." He thought.

He answered the door to find his cousin looking around. He wondered what she could want.

"Have you seen my mother?" She asked.
"No." He replied.

She wasn't convinced. Tim appeared on edge around her. His cousin became curious about what Tim was hiding.

"Well, I'm looking for her." She said.
"Look somewhere else." He said.

His cousin thought for a few short seconds while she tried to figure things out in her head.

"I could have sworn she said she was coming here to look for her sister a few moments ago." She said.
"Not here." He said.

She was confused. Her mother never lied to her and she told her where she was going earlier.

"Are you sure?" She asked.
"Yes." He replied.

After looking behind Tim, his cousin saw the empty house. She curiously began questioning him.

"Are you selling your house?" She asked.
"Yes, I have already moved. I am just finishing up on some cleaning and I'm leaving." He replied.

This surprised her to hear. Tim had not said anything to the family before about moving.

"How come you haven't told anyone?" She asked.

He was beginning to get frustrated with her. Tim felt she should mind her own business.

"I didn't know I was required to tell everyone what I do in life. I can live it the way I want." He replied.
"I don't like the attitude you always have. If you see my mother, let me know." She said.

Tim finished his cleaning fast and left. He wanted to get out of there before anyone else stopped by to question him.

"I forgot to kill her!" He thought.

It was too late to turn back now. Darkness was falling and he needed to get home for dinner.

"I'll go back in a few days and finish her off. She will be fine until I get back." He thought.

Tim got to the point where he didn't care anymore. He figured he would go back later to bury his aunt's body after she had a few days to die.

"I'll bury her next to my mother. They can live happily together on the other side." He thought.

Continuing with his killings, Tim murdered three other women to add to his collection out in the victim graveyard. He was supposed to lay low, but they fell into his arms. Two of them he ran into while hiking through the woods. This he enjoyed daily to stay in shape. The women were so innocent to have their lives taken early. Unfortunately, they were in the right place at the wrong time. Tim couldn't control his urge to kill anymore.

"I had to kill them. Each and every one." He thought while at his graveyard one day.

The third woman, he met while at the store shopping for food. This was an easy opportunity for him. Her car broke down and he offered her a ride home with her groceries. Except, he killed her instead and took her groceries to the cabin with his. Tim became so wrapped up in his killings, that he forgot about leaving his aunt tied up. Now, he would have to sneak over at night to bury her.

"I have to bury her before anyone finds her and suspects me. I can't take the risk." He thought.

He was relaxed one evening watching television when a special alert came through. His aunt had broken free from him tying her up and went to the police. Now, he would be exposed to the world. Tim would have to give his old house up and abandon it for good to never return again. His family was on television also, pleading for him to give himself up. *Would Tim decide to turn himself in?* It had appeared that everyone was searching for him, but he couldn't be found.

"They will never find me out here. I'm hidden well and no one knows where I live now." He thought.

Tim knew at this point he couldn't be seen anymore by anyone. He spent the next three years living his life in nature away from everyone. The police searched for a long time, but it all came to a dead end. Tim kept up with the news stations while he went on about his daily life. Every once in a while, they would post his picture to the world. He would never reveal himself.

"They are still looking for me? I have gained a lot of popularity." He would think to himself.

While he stayed hidden for quite some time, there had been no more killings. His urges were there, but he had to tuck them away. During the three years, Tim visited his victim's graveyard once a week to reflect on his life. Memories of his killings stayed in his thoughts.

"I wish I would have had a different mother. My life would have been better." He thought.

Still blaming his mother for what had happened, Tim would never be able to let that go. Often, he thought about what his life could have been like if he was born into a different family. No one he went to school with had turned into a killer. His cousins even seemed to have good lives. Everywhere he looked, Tim saw happiness. *Was he the only one who was going through a situation like his?*

"Life has never been fair to me. Why couldn't destiny give me a better life?" He thought.

There was no way he could change anything now. He knew that the police would find him sooner or later. Nothing would stop his destiny from happening. Tim would get what he deserved in time. Other days, he spent in his hidden cave deep in the woods. He loved it there. This helped pass his time during his lonely moments. *Would he soon become too lonely and want to kill again?*

Tim learned quickly how to adapt to his nature life without outside help. He had enough food stored to live off of for a long while, along with his garden that he took care of daily. In the winter, he kept warm by building fires from the wood he collected during the fall months. On occasion, he would hunt animals to kill for meat. Whatever he had to do, Tim made a way to survive.

"I don't need the world." He thought.

To help with his urge to kill, sometimes Tim would capture animals and tie them up pretending they were women. Even the fight with them was challenging at times. He tortured some of them before he cut their heads off. Keeping the heads as a trophy, Tim would bury them. He created a new graveyard for the animals separate from his victim graveyard. Using carved wood pieces as a grave marking, Tim wanted it to be different than the original graveyard he had for women. Even so, both yards would be unique in their own way.

"This is perfect." He thought as he observed everything.

Tim showed a lot of mental issues from his past. In one way or another, he would live a satisfying life. The world couldn't stop him. If he stayed hidden, no one would figure it out. With his parents gone, Tim never had to worry about them wanting to visit. To him, he had no family. Tim got rid of his cell phone when he first went into hiding. There was no communication with the world he had once known unless he left the woods.

"I can stay hidden forever." He thought.

Over time, his looks changed. He let his hair grow long and grew a beard. He dressed in rags like a homeless person.

"No one will recognize me now." He thought.

It was only a matter of time before Tim began thinking about leaving the woods to get another victim. With the way his looks had changed, he thought he was unrecognizable. *Would someone catch him out?* Tim knew he would be taking a big risk, but he had to decide if it was a risk he was willing to take. With the loneliness, he needed to get away from the woods for a short time.

"I'm getting very tempted." He thought.

The animal killings were becoming a bore to him. Watching the news daily, Tim noticed the story about the serial killer had died down after a few years. Everyone had assumed that maybe he died.

"Let them believe I died. I will surprise them one day when I come out of hiding." He thought.

The police weren't so convinced. They had a feeling that the killer was in hiding and would come out eventually to start killing again. Tim thought the discussions about him were interesting. Sometimes, he would sit on the hillside in the woods by the walking path to hear what others had to say.

"She looks like a good victim." He thought.

As he sat and watched women pass, Tim kept control not to go after them. This was hard for him since his last killing had been a few years. Each day he watched made it more difficult. One afternoon, Tim couldn't hold back. With no one else in sight, he attacked a woman walking alone. Then, dragged her body into the woods back to his cabin so no one would know. Thinking smart, he would start burning his victims and burying their bones in his victim graveyard.

"How will the police know now?" He thought.

This continued for months. Now, the police had a handful of missing women cases in the area to deal with instead of murder cases. They questioned if it was the same man that had done the killings, except this time he wasn't leaving their bodies lying around.

17

One afternoon, Tim was outside his cabin when he heard a noise coming from his food storage shed.

"An animal is trying to get into my food. I'll sneak up on it quietly so it doesn't hear me." He thought.

Moving closer, Tim had a stick in his hand to scare the animal away. Once he approached the shed, Tim saw an older child. He wondered why she was snooping through his food.

"What are you doing here!" He said angrily.

The girl became fearful at first. She stood in shock not knowing how to respond to Tim's yelling.

"I was hungry." She mumbled.
"Don't your parents feed you?" He asked.
"I'm eighteen now. My father kicked me out of the house. I don't have a place to go." She said.

Feeling sorry for the girl, Tim made her some food. As they were eating, the girl began to talk more.

"You have a nice place out here." She said.
"Thanks." Tim said.

Tim continued eating as the girl kept talking. She was happy to meet someone out in the woods.

"I've been around here for a few weeks now checking everything out, but I haven't seen you until today." She said.

Now, Tim was a little curious. He wondered how he missed not seeing her on his property.

"Where have you been sleeping?" He asked.
"Deep in the woods. On occasion, I sneak up here for a few cans of food." She replied.
"So, you have been stealing my food?" He asked.

Hesitantly, the girl spoke.

"Yes. I'm sorry." She replied.
"I thought it was the animals." He said.

Tim thought for a few moments. He wanted to help her in some way. This wasn't like him at all.

"Look, I have a cave out there. It has food storage and it would be a place you could stay for a while if you want." He suggested.
"Oh! That would be great!" She excitedly said.

After a few seconds,

"I have one rule." He said.

The girl glanced at him curiously. She wanted to know what stipulations he was going to set for her.

"What's that?" She asked.
"No one can ever know about my cave." He replied.

She thought for a few seconds.

"I won't take anyone there." She said.
"Good." He said.

Tim took her out to the cave and settled her in for the evening. She looked around for a few moments.

"This is amazing." She said.

She observed the cave while Tim reminded her of the rules she needed to follow.

"Never bring anyone here." He said.
"I won't." She said.

He began to walk away. Wanting to relax, Tim needed to return home before nightfall.

"Where are you going?" She asked.
"Back to my cabin." He replied.

She was grateful for his help.

"Thanks for helping me." She said.

Continuing to walk away, he only had one more question for her that was on his mind.

"What is your name?" He asked.
"Suzy." She replied.

Tim smiled.

"I'm Tim." he said.
"Cool name." She said.

She smiled back as Tim walked away.

"I'll see you tomorrow." He said.

On the way back to the cabin, Tim thought about the girl. She was too young to be out on her own in the wilderness. Maybe he could teach her some survival skills. *Did Tim have a soft heart for the girl?* Over the next few months, Tim and Suzy became friends. They explored the woods and walked creeks. Suzy was a nature lover also, so they were very compatible when it came to a friendship. Despite the age difference, they got along great together. Life went well for a while.

"This is exactly what I needed." Tim thought.

One evening, Tim decided to turn the television on to see if news had died down about him.

"I haven't watched the news in a while. Let's see if there's any new information." Tim said to himself.

A news alert came on as he switched channels. A picture of his new friend Suzy was put across the screen. Tim was curious about what was going on.

"Why is her picture on the news?" He wondered.

Suzy was wanted by the police for a crime she had committed. It appeared that there was a warrant for her arrest for not showing up to court.

"She lied to me." Tim thought.

Tim knew Suzy put him at risk by lying. He could get in trouble if the police knew he had been hiding her out. Not having a choice, Tim had to make her leave. The police were already suspicious of him for the killings, so he didn't need this problem on him too. Suzy would have to figure her issues out on her own without Tim's help anymore. This new information discouraged him.

"She should have been honest with me from the beginning instead of being secretive." Tim thought.

He was never one who liked for anyone to keep secrets from him. His mother learned the hard way. If Suzy wouldn't leave, she would be risking her life. She didn't know Tim was a killer. When they explored the woods, Tim was careful not to take her near his graveyards.

The next morning, Tim ventured off to the cave to confront Suzy. When he arrived, she wasn't there.

"Where could she be?" He asked himself.

After a while of searching, Tim had no clue where Suzy was. He headed back toward the cabin. He decided to stop to check on his victims' sites on the way. As he approached the graveyard, he saw Suzy glancing around.

"What are you doing here?" Tim asked.

Suzy turned around quickly.

"I wanted to explore this side of the woods." She said.
"You are not supposed to be here." He said.
"What is this place?" She asked.

Tim became upset.

"When were you going to tell me the truth?" He asked.

Suzy looked at Tim in confusion.

"About what?" She asked.
"Your dad didn't kick you out." He claimed.

She was shocked to hear him say this.

"How do you know?" She asked.
"I watched the news last night." He replied.

Suzy stood in silence.

"You are going to have to leave." He said.
"Why?" She asked.
"It's too risky for you to be here." He replied.

She thought for a few moments.

"Where am I going to go?" She asked.
"That's not my problem. You are a fugitive on the run. I can't be involved in that." He replied.

Suzy began to walk away when she suddenly tripped on a stone. She quickly observed it.

"Put it down!" Tim hollered.

She quickly threw it to the ground.

"These look like miniature headstones." She said.
"You need to leave." Tim said.

Suzy stood to her feet as she gazed at Tim.

"Do you have something buried here?" She asked.

She glanced around more as Tim stood in silence.

"Is this a graveyard?" She asked.

Tim began taking small steps toward Suzy.

"What if it is?" He asked.

Suzy became nervous.

"What do you have buried here?" She asked.
"Pictures of my victims mostly." He replied.

This startled Suzy.

"What do you mean?" She asked.

They glared into each other's eyes.

"Didn't you watch all the news that was going around before you came here?" He asked.
"You are the killer they have been looking for." She replied.
"Yes." He said.

Suzy took a few steps back as Tim let out a soft laugh.

"You never thought you would be standing face-to-face with a serial killer one day, did you?" He asked.
"You helped me though." She replied.
"Yes, I did." He said.

She looked confused.

"Why didn't you kill me?" She asked.
"I had no need to kill you until now." He replied.

Suzy began to run through the woods. Tim ran behind her. He knew he wouldn't let her get away.

"You can't outrun me." He said.

Suzy ran faster.
"Leave me alone!" She yelled out.

Eventually, they ended up in the cave. Suzy ran inside to hide. Tim stopped at the entrance to catch his breath.

"I know this cave like the back of my hand. She can't hide from me." He whispered to himself.

After entering the cave, Tim glanced around.

"I will find you." He hollered.

His voice echoed through the cave. He knew Suzy could hear him. It was only a matter of time before she would be part of his victim graveyard with the other women he killed.

"Suzy, where are you." He whispered out.

All of a sudden, he heard a noise. Suzy was hiding in a dark corner of the cave. Tim approached her slowly.

"Don't hurt me." Suzy said.
"I have to." Tim said.

Tim gently put his hand around her neck.

"I won't tell anyone." She pleaded.
"You lied to me before. I can't trust you." He said.

He began squeezing her neck slightly.

"Please, I will do anything." She pleaded more.
"There is nothing you can say or do that will save you." He responded.

Tim strangled Suzy until she took her last breath. There would be no sexual picture since she was so young. Tim didn't have urges in that way toward her. Instead, he was just going to bury her body.

"It's such a long way back to the graveyard to drag a body. I'll bury her here in the cave." He said to himself.

Tim dug a hole in the dirt floor of the cave and put Suzy's body in it. He admired her for a moment before covering her with dirt to bury her. He remembered all the fun times they had in just a few short months. Tim hated that everything had to end the way it did. He returned to his cabin to clean up, eat, and go to bed for the night. It would be a fresh start for him the next morning.

18

After many more months in the woods, Tim became bored with the lonely life. He decided to venture away from the woods for a bit. It had been a while since he heard anything on the news about his killings.

"They probably forgot all about me by now." He thought.

Glancing over his treasure graveyard one day, his cravings began to grow. The memories of each victim flooded through his mind. It became unbearable. He wanted more.

"I have to get out of these woods for the day." He thought.

After a night of planning, Tim left the woods the next morning. He walked the streets freely around town. Enjoying his time out, Tim didn't think anyone would notice him. While eating at a restaurant for lunch, he observed a guy walking around staring at him. As he continued to eat, the man whispered to his friends. Tim thought it was time he left.

"Maybe he recognizes me." Tim thought.

He walked the streets once more. Suddenly, he glanced over to see people looking at him.

"I need to get out of here." He said to himself.

Tim continued walking until he was back in his woods.

"That was too risky." He thought.

He knew the risks were too high to wander the streets. Tim would forever be stuck living the cabin life alone. What he wasn't aware of, one man who recognized him on television had followed him home. The man was careful not to be seen or heard. Someone now knew Tim's location without being known. This information would be taken to the police. After he reported everything to the cops, it was only a matter of time before they would raid Tim. It would take time for the police to catch him, but they worked night and day for an arrest now that they knew where he was.

In the meantime, Tim was working on another kill for his victim's graveyard. He had no knowledge the police were on his tail and would soon be raiding his private property. One day while walking to the trails, Tim noticed a woman sitting on a log. He approached her with caution.

"May I help you with something?" He asked.

Startled, the woman turned to look.

"Who are you?" She asked.
"I'm the owner of this property." Tim replied.

The woman quickly stood to her feet.

"I'm sorry to trespass." She said.
"What are you doing here?" He asked.
"I must have wandered off the trail too far." She replied.

After a few moments, Tim decided to offer assistance.

"Let me help you find your way." He offered.
"That would be great." She said.

The two of them walked together through the woods. Tim politely showed her back to the trails.

"Thank you." She said.

"Maybe you can come back to visit sometime." Tim stated as the woman walked off in a hurry.

"Yes, I will. See you later." She said.

Over the next few weeks, there was no sign of the woman. Tim became discouraged as he walked back toward his cabin.

"Nice place you have here." A woman spoke.

Tim looked up quickly to see the new woman standing there.

"I didn't think you would ever return." He said.
"I'm here." She said.
"I see." He said.

After a few moments,

"Aren't you going to invite me in?" She asked.
"Where are my manners." He replied.

Tim let the new woman in his cabin. This was not typical for him to do. He was a private person but was caught up in his urges at the moment. He made the woman a quick meal, and they sat together for a conversation.

"Why are you out here alone?" She asked.
"Just needed my space." He replied.

They sat eating for a couple more minutes.

"Do you work?" She asked.
"On occasion." He replied.

She waited for him to talk about his job, but he continued eating. She could tell he was a private person.

"What kind of work do you do?" She asked.
"Photography." He replied.

She was surprised to hear this.

"What do you do?" He asked.
"I am a teacher." She replied.
"Oh." He responded.

After eating, they went for a walk and talked more. Both grew interested in each other. She left that day promising to return soon. Over the next few months, the two of them began a relationship. Tim showed her around the property and shared stories of the survival life he had been living. She told him stories about her teaching days and the lifestyles she had lived over time. They seemed very compatible.

"She is what I want." Tim thought.

The police were just about ready to go in for an arrest. They had a day planned for everything and were in the process of getting things situated. Tim still had no idea the police knew where he was.

His urges remained throughout their relationship. He learned to control them around her. Tim wanted to gain her trust because she had seemed like a strong one. This kill had to be right. One evening at dinner, she told Tim about a dream she had.

"I had the weirdest dream about you." She said.

This caught his attention.

"What was the dream about?" He asked.
"You were chasing me through the woods." She replied.

Tim looked confused.

"Why was I chasing you?" He asked.
"I don't know. I just remember being really scared." She replied.

This concerned Tim.

"There is something I haven't told you." She said.
"What is that?" He asked.

She paused for a short few seconds.

"I have a little psychic side to me." She said.
"What do you mean?" He asked.
"I sometimes have revealing dreams of things that are going to happen." She replied.

Shocked, Tim stared at her. If she learned about him, he would have to kill her in some way.

"I think you should leave." Tim said.

She looked at him with confusion.

"Okay." She said.

Not asking questions, she left in silence. It was a couple of days before Tim saw her again.

"Hi." She said as she walked on his porch.
"What are you doing here?" He asked.
"I was concerned about the other night." She replied.

Tim continued to swing on his porch.

"Look, I know how disturbing everything sounded." She said.
"I didn't find it disturbing." He said.

She looked at him with confusion.

"What do you mean?" She asked.
"Maybe your dream was telling you something." He replied.

This concerned her.

"What would it be telling me?" She asked.
"Maybe it was warning you of me." He replied.
"You don't seem like a hurtful person." She said.

They both continued to stare at each other.

"There is a lot you don't know about me." He said.
"Tell me." She said.
"Let me show you something." He said.

Tim started walking towards the woods.

"Where are we going?" She asked.
"Follow me." He replied as he kept walking.

After a few moments, the woman stopped.

"I'm not going any farther until you tell me what is going on." She said.

He turned around. They stood face to face.

"I want to show you what I am." He said.
"Why can't you tell me?" She asked.

"You will understand once you see." He replied.

She looked at him hesitantly speaking.

"I don't have a good feeling about this. Something is telling me not to go." She said.

Tim began to laugh quietly.

"What's funny?" She asked.
"You want me to tell you?" He asked.
"Yes." She replied.

After a moment, Tim explained who he was.

"I am a killer." He bluntly said.
"Is this a joke?" She asked.
"No." He replied.

Shocked, she wasn't sure how to respond.

"I was going to show you my graveyard." He said.
"You have women buried here?" She asked.
"Just one out in my cave. I'm a photographer, so I take pictures of my women after I strangle them." Tim explained.

The woman was overwhelmed by all this information.

"Wait, I did burn a woman too. Her bones are in the graveyard." He continued.

Why was Tim confessing these things to her? Tim planned to kill the woman, so he didn't hold back. *Who would she tell if she were dead?* He had no concern in his mind at the moment. Grabbing at the woman, she started to fight him off. There was a short struggle before he gained control. With one hand around her neck slightly, she pleaded for her life.

"Please, let me go. I won't tell anyone." She said.

Tim smiled with enjoyment.

"That's what they all say before they die." He stated.

As he began to strangle her to death, he heard shouting behind him. Tim turned to see cops running toward him.

"Let go of her!"
"Put your hands in the air!"
"Step away from her now!"

He was in shock at what was happening. The police had caught him in action. There was no denying he was the killer they had searched for all this time. *What would happen to Tim now?* They cuffed him while they got medical attention to the woman. A few seconds more, she wouldn't have made it. The ambulance drove off with her to the hospital. The police drove off with Tim to the station for questioning.

"We have been looking for you a while now." The detective said.

Tim sat in silence not wanting to talk to the police. They read him his rights. He denied wanting to speak, so they put him in a holding cell until further questioning. Even though he was caught red-handed, Tim had no interest in telling them anything. A mate next to him started a conversation.

"What are you in for?" The mate asked.

After a few seconds,

"Cat got your tongue?" The mate asked.

Tim slowly turned his head toward him.

"Mind your business." He said.
"That attitude won't get you far in jail." The mate responded.

Neither talked again to each other. Tim waited patiently to see what would come next for him.

19

The next morning, detectives moved Tim to a private room where they could talk to him. The room was a decent size with a big wall mirror. Tim started thinking about what he had done. Suddenly, a detective walked in and sat down. The questioning began.

"Why did you do it?" The detective asked.
"Do what?" Tim asked.

The detective was quite annoyed with Tim. He didn't have time for the mind playing.

"Look, we both know why you are here. You can either stop with the games or we can go straight to trial." The detective explained.

Tim grew a smirk on his face. So far, the detective hadn't shown him anything that said he killed anyone.

"You can't prove I did anything." Tim stated.

The detective held the file in the air. Tim became quiet while he observed the file.

"I have more evidence than you think." The detective responded.
"Show me." Tim said.

After a few seconds, the detective slammed the file onto the table. This made Tim a little nervous.

"Did you forget that your last attack is a witness of your confession?" The detective asked.

Tim sat silently glaring into the detective's eyes. He knew the confession would hold up in court.

"Remember, you admitted that you killed several women to her." The detective said.

He continued speaking as Tim sat patiently listening to what the detective was saying.

"As a matter of fact, right this minute we have police searching your graveyard." The detective said.

Being concerned, Tim never opened his mouth. He wasn't happy about anyone being on his property.

"So, why did you do it?" The detective asked once more.
"You would never understand." Tim replied.

The detective wanted more information. He needed a confession from Tim, but knew it would be hard to get.

"How many have you killed?" The detective asked.
"Too many." Tim replied.

This made the detective curious. He wasn't sure if Tim had killed more than they knew.

"What's too many?" The detective asked.
"I want a lawyer." Tim replied.

Even though he wanted to continue, the detective knew he had to stop and let Tim consult a lawyer at that point. After talking to Tim, the detective realized there may have been more potential victims than he realized. He waited for the results of the search to come back.

In the meantime, back at Tim's land, the police were working to find as much evidence as possible to use against Tim. They were busy digging up the animal graveyard. One officer spoke to another.

"This is disturbing."
"Why would he mutilate these animals in this way?"

A detective in charge approached the two officers. He was eager to find anything for a prosecution.

"Have you found anything?" The detective asked.
"All we have found here is a graveyard of dead animals." One officer replied.

All of a sudden, another officer in the distance hollered out. The detective glanced over.

"Detective! You might want to come over here and take a look at this!"

He walked over to the other grave sites. Curiosity grew within to see something.

"What is it?" The detective asked.
"We are finding pictures in this graveyard." The officer said.

The detective couldn't believe what he was looking at. It was great evidence for their case.

"Apparently, he took photos posing his victims." The officer stated.
"Bag these for evidence." The detective said.

Suddenly, another officer had more details to share with the detective at the moment.

"I found bones in this grave." He said.

The detective approached the grave observing. He knelt beside the shallow grave.

"These are human bones." He said.
"They look burned." The officer said.

He thought for a few moments.

"I remember a fire pit up by the cabin. Search it good." The detective ordered.

Eventually, they completed their search and returned to the station with bags full of evidence. Now, Tim couldn't deny the killings. After they processed all the evidence, Tim was questioned again.

"Why am I here again?" Tim asked.

The detective placed the photos onto the table of all the evidence they found at Tim's property.

"Can you tell me about these?" The detective asked.

Tim observed the photos in deep thought. This took him back to his killing moments.

"Tim?" The detective responded.
"These are my victims." Tim answered.
"So, you killed them all?" The detective asked.
"Yes." Tim replied.

He couldn't believe Tim had confessed. After a few moments, the detective continued.

"Did you know the victims?" The detective asked.
"No." Tim quietly replied.

Tim knew he was caught. So, he began to cooperate with the police. There was no more hiding the fact that he killed all these women. He thought nothing mattered at this point as to what he would say. When asked why he killed those women, Tim explained his life story and what led to the way he felt. It wouldn't get him freed for his crimes though.

"Are there any other victims besides these?" The detective asked.
"Yes." Tim replied.

Tim confessed to everything and even told police where his other victims were, including his mother. With the truth out, Tim didn't feel any better than before he was arrested. They took him back to his jail cell. He awaited court for a few weeks. When the day finally arrived, they put shackles and handcuffs on him. Then, escorted him to court. As he walked in, Tim saw that a lot of people had attended.

"Who are these people?" Tim asked quietly.
"These are the family of all your victims." The officer replied.

Surprised, Tim had no sorrow for his crimes.

"What do you plead?" The judge asked.
"Guilty, guilty, guilty." Tim replied sarcastically.

The judge looked concerned about the way Tim was acting. He began questioning the prosecution.

"Is he fit to make a plea?" The judge asked.
"Yes, I am!" Tim hollered.
"Your honor, He has confessed to everything and is fit to stand for his sentencing hearing." The prosecution replied.

The judge thought for a few seconds.

"Kill him!" The people shouted.
"Order in this court!" The judge shouted.

Everyone became quiet.

"I want a mental evaluation done and put on my desk before the sentencing hearing. Court adjourned." The judge stated.

He pleaded guilty to all the killings. The case never had to go to trial. Another court date was set for the sentencing. Tim was put in protected custody while awaiting the next court date. A month passed before he was taken for his evaluation. He was escorted by several police guards. As he walked down the hallway, everyone stared at him. He was the number one discussion from everyone in the jail.

Tim walked slowly into a room where he met the doctor who would evaluate him.

"State your name." The doctor said.
"Timothy." He responded.
"Have a seat." The doctor said.

Sitting in front of the doctor, Tim was intimidated.

"Why do you think you're here today?" The doctor asked.
"Because I killed people." Tim replied.
"Did you know you were killing them?" The doctor asked.
"Yes, I chose them." Tim replied.

Confused, the doctor continued.

"Explain how you chose them." The doctor said.
"I walked the streets until I felt it was the right one. Then, I followed them before going in for the kill." Tim explained.

This wasn't his first rodeo, but the doctor was surprised by Tim's reactions to the questions. It was as if he was satisfied with what he had done. Tim showed no remorse.

"What happened that you felt the need to kill an innocent person?" The doctor asked.
"I was angry." Tim replied.
"What made you angry?" The doctor asked.

Tim was hesitant for a moment.

"My mother for lying to me my whole life, and seeing people around me happy." Tim replied.

The doctor realized Tim was insane, but knew what he was doing at the time of his killings.

"How did you feel after you killed someone?" The doctor asked.
"I felt relieved." Tim replied.

Tim never learned coping skills for his problems. Instead, he resorted right away to killing someone. He sat through a series of questions before being taken back to his cell. Walking up the long hallway, he smiled at the passing officers.

Jail life was extreme for Tim. He sat in a cell all day with very little light shining in. He had no social time with anyone. Tim was given food but hardly ate any of it. Anger grew by the day. The loneliness was hard on him. What he would have given to become free again.

"I have to get out of here." Tim thought.

He knew there wasn't a chance to get out of jail. He tried to hang himself with a sheet, but he would soon be rescued. The officers eventually removed everything except a mattress from his cell. Once a week, he was escorted to a shower. This was the most freedom he received from his cell.

"Maybe I can plan an escape." He thought.

There were too many guards at his cell door for Tim to escape. Someone was always watching. One morning, Tim was allowed a visitor. He assumed it was his lawyer, but when he entered the room, he couldn't believe who he was looking at. Ava had decided to come to see him. She had to get permission from the courts first. Tim grew excited inside for the first time in a long time. This was his first social interaction in months, besides with officers.

"How did you get to see me?" Tim asked.
"The judge granted the visit." Ava replied.
"How are you?" She asked.

Tim sighed.

"Insane in here. Get me out of here." Tim replied.
"I wish I could, but I can't." She said.
"I know." Tim said.

They talked for about twenty minutes before the officers told them time was up. Ava was sad that things had to end this way. She would have loved to have a brother to hang out with. Tim wasn't happy that he was living the jail life now. *Did he have regrets for killing?* No. He only had regrets for being careless and getting caught.

"I would kill again if given the chance." Tim thought.

He would most likely be locked up for the rest of his life with no chance of parole. Tim would probably die in jail. He couldn't hurt anyone now.

20

One afternoon, Tim was escorted for his weekly shower by two officers. One was a male, the other female.

"This is different." Tim thought.

Usually, it was two male officers. For some reason, this time a female was involved. Tim's urges grew as he stared at the female officer. If he tried to go after her, he knew she would be stronger with the training she had. He had to be careful and quick.

During his shower, he thought more about her. The male officer left the restroom as Tim exited the shower. Getting dressed, Tim could hear a conversation between them. He listened closely.

"Dang." The male said.
"What's wrong?" The female asked.
"I'll be right back. I have to assist with an inmate fight." The male officer said to the female officer.

The female was hesitant for a few seconds. After thinking about it, she grew confident.

"Go. I can handle this scumbag." The female said.
"Don't let your guard down." The male said as he ran away.

The female officer was left alone with Tim. She figured her partner would be back before Tim finished his shower. Tim heard this and thought it would be a good opportunity to attack her.

"I'm already in jail. I might as well make the best of it." He thought.

Taking the opportunity to go in for the kill, Tim came around the corner quickly and grabbed the officer around the neck putting her to sleep. She never had time to react.

"I'm good at this." Tim complimented himself.

Tim dragged her into the showers. He knew he had to work fast before the other officer returned. He ripped her pants off and raped her. She began to wake up, but Tim put her back to sleep until he was finished. He continued to do this every time she woke up.

"That was so satisfying." He thought.

Wrapping his hands around her neck tightly, Tim strangled the officer until she took her last breath. At about that moment, he heard screaming behind him. He turned to see the male officer had returned.

"Get away from her!" He shouted as he lounged toward Tim.

The male officer pushed Tim to the ground and put him in cuffs. He called for backup and then attended to the female officer beginning CPR. He wanted to save her.

"Come on. Don't die on me." The officer said.

Tim watched while still cuffed on the ground. He could have easily attacked the male officer too, but he didn't.

"It's too late for her." Tim said.
"Why did you do this to her?" The male officer cried out.

"I needed to satisfy my urge." Tim replied.
"You're sick." The officer stress-fully said.

Tim smiled at the male officer. He had a short enjoyment that he would never forget.

"Come on, breath." The male said while still applying CPR.
"You are wasting your time." Tim said.
"Shut up!" the officer yelled.
"Okay." Tim said sarcastically.

More officers came running in. Now, Tim knew he would get extra time added for the kill.

"What happened?" An officer shouted.
"He's killed her." The male said.

The officer was confused.

"How did this happen?" The officer said.
"I left her for a few minutes. I shouldn't have left her." The male cried.

Tim continued to keep the situation escalating. He was having his fun moments while he could.

"I raped and killed her." He said with happiness.

Officers began standing Tim to his feet. They heard him confess to the murder.

"Get him out of here!" The male officer shouted.

Returning to his cell, Tim felt a deep sense of satisfaction. He took a deep breath of relief. The female officer was pronounced dead at the scene. As hard as the male tried to save her, Tim had done too much damage with the strangulation. No one could save her.

The male felt horrible for leaving her alone with such an insane person. This should have never happened. He blamed himself for not being there to protect his partner from the monster Tim was.

The sentencing hearing approached quickly. Tim walked into court again cuffed and shackled. The judge already knew about the killing before the court hearing.

"Why would you kill an officer?" The judge asked.
"What did I have to lose?" Tim asked.
"Your life." The judge said.
"I have already lost that by being in here." Tim said.

The judge looked at Tim in disgust. Tim risked everything because he had already lost his life.

"I enjoyed every minute of it." Tim stated.
"You disgust me." The judge said.

Being in court in front of a judge who held your fate, Tim had no care for what he said.

"I've heard enough!" The judge said loudly.

More charges were added to Tim's sentencing. The judge ordered the Death sentence for Tim. He would be put to death by lethal injection. Tim was under strict watch until his death date. He wasn't allowed to leave his cell for any reason. Being set to die in just a few short weeks, Tim concentrated on his killings one last time. He was satisfied with what he had done.

"I have lived a fulfilling miserable life." He thought to himself.

He still blamed his mother and knew she was probably waiting for him on the other side.

"That's going to be the worst punishment. Seeing her again." He thought.

On the last day in jail before his death, Tim got a visitor from his cousins. They gave the family time to visit before his lethal injection to say their goodbyes.

"I don't want any visitors." Tim said to the officers.
"Are you sure?" The officer asked.
"Yes." Tim replied quickly.

The officer reminded him this would be his last chance to make amends with his family before he died.

"You do know this will be your last time to see family?" The officer said.
"I don't want to see any of my family." Tim replied.
"Okay. I will let them know." The officer said as he walked away.

Tim didn't care if he ever saw his family again. Being in that family was what made him the way he was. Now, he had to figure out how to avoid his mother in the next life.

"I hope the next life is better than this one has been." He thought.

Tim thought all night about how the afterlife would be. The next morning, he was taken to the execution room. He was put in a chair waiting for his death time. The room had a bed with medical equipment around it. There was also a big window that had a curtain.

"What is that window?" He asked.
"We will open the curtain when it's time." The worker replied.

Tim was confused, He had never seen an execution. So, he wanted to know things.

"What's behind the curtain?" Tim asked.
"The victim's family and your family." The worker replied.

Tim didn't like hearing this.

"Why are they all here?" He asked.
"To watch you die." The worker replied.

Tim was angry.

"Tell them to leave." He said.
"You killed someone in their family. They have every right to be here." The worker explained.

Tim had to think fast.

"Then I don't want the curtain opened." Tim said.
"That's not a choice you have." The worker said.
"Why not?" Tim asked.
"Because you are a murderer. What you want doesn't matter." The worker said.

They moved Tim to the bed and hooked him up to IV. He grew extremely nervous at that point. His life began to flash before his eyes as he stayed in deep thought.

"I will be dead in a few minutes." He thought.

Suddenly, the curtains opened. Tim glanced over to see everyone staring at him. They all wanted justice and would get it in just a short time.

"Do you have any last words?" The worker asked.

Tim looked at the families giving them an evil eye as he smiled with enjoyment from all of his accomplishments.

"No." He said happily.

The families were distraught by his looks. They wanted this to end, for Tim to not kill another victim. Ava had never seen the evil part of Tim. She grew scared by the way he reacted toward the victim's families.

"I was lucky that I wasn't one of his victims." Ava thought.

Ava counted her blessings. She could have easily been killed by Tim if he had wanted to. She felt lucky to be alive in the moment. Feeling sorry for the families, she continued to watch while they finished prepping Tim for his execution. This would be the day her brother died.

"Why did he get the killer's blood and not me?" Ava thought.

Maybe it had to do with the male dominance of the family. Males seem stronger than females. Ava was afraid that if she ever had a boy child, it could carry the killer gene too.

"I'm never having kids." Ava thought.

As the worker approached Tim with the needle, He grew scared. For the first time in a long time, Tim had a scared feeling. Tim jerked his body.

"It won't help to fight at this point." The worker said.
"Leave me alone." Tim squirmed.
"Lie still and things will go faster." The worker said.

His cousins were talking on the other side of the window. They hated to see Tim die.

"I can't believe he was the killer." A first said.
"It's a shame." A second said.
"His whole life thrown away." A third said.
"He brought this onto himself." A fourth said.

Hearing them talk, Ava began to cry. She couldn't hold back her sadness. Even though she only knew Tim for a short time, Ava cared for him a lot.

"I love you." She whispered softly as she watched.

The fluid in the needle was injected slowly. Tim looked at Ava as he was dying. His vision began to fade away. His heart suddenly stopped. He felt a rush of pain before he finally died. He left the world he hated. Tim would no longer be able to hurt anyone again.

Tears ran down Ava's face. It was hard for her to watch. Afterward, everyone left while they took Tim's body away.

"What will they do with his body?" Ava asked an officer.
"It will be cremated. You can pick up his ashes in a few days." The officer replied.
"Okay." Ava said.

Ava thought for a few moments longer before she left. It was like leaving a piece of her behind.

"This is so hard." Ava thought.

She collected his ashes when they were available.

"What am I going to do with these?" She thought.

She put the ashes in a box and sealed it up. Ava would keep them hidden in her attic. She would eventually find a way to get past her heartache and move on in life. This would be a story that everyone around the world talked about for generations. Tim would always be known as the *"Estranged Photographer"* serial killer.

The Rejected

Betrayal of life,
Separation from society,
Deep within our self,
Comes with a lot of anxiety.

Emotional wounds,
Disconnection of feelings,
Each day often brings,
A large number of dealings.

Anger and Fear,
Darkens the days,
Holding onto hope,
May grow with age.

Destruction of affection,
Trauma and sorrow,
Somewhere there has to be,
A better tomorrow.

www.ingramcontent.com/pod-product-compliance
Lightning Source LLC
LaVergne TN
LVHW021818060526
838201LV00058B/3433